PRAISE FROM MORE BY

JAMES CASPER

I0567861

These characters were real. They were people with mannerisms and flyaway hair and quirky little habits.

— SARAH REINHARD

When I read *Everywhere in Chains* last winter, I actually read it twice because when I got to the end the first time, I wasn't ready to say goodbye to Penelope and Felix—they're my favorite.

— SR. MARIA GORETTI

The book was well written and fast paced and believable. The ending is surprising. Very enjoyable. Not gory or and no foul language—a pleasant change.

— AMAZON REVIEWER

THE ZODIAC CLUB

A CONSTELLATION OF STORIES

JAMES CASPER

Co-Editor
KATE CASPER
Co-Editor
RACHEL WHY

FARHAVEN PRESS

In Memory of Uncle Bob
and other unsung heroes of forgotten pathways.

CONTENTS

FOREWORD

This collection of short stories by James Casper takes you into the lives of people struggling to be understood. While that can seem a dire subject—and is much of the time—some of these stories will make you laugh out loud.

In the title story, a woman holding an exclusive club in her home sees no reason to justify her open affair with one of the chosen members; her husband comes up with some strange means of coping.

In another story, a hardworking man raises his wife's illegitimate child while dreaming of a better life.

In a third tale, a man who is happiest left

alone is thrown into the spotlight of a comet that shames his reputation.

In yet another, a couple who have always gotten along well are not able to be together when the end comes.

People trying to get things right, people trying to make things right, people hoping there is a way for everything to turn out right in the end.

In Casper's beautiful prose, characters become real people you invest in and root for, laugh about and cry about. Filled with rich description and timed just right to keep you wondering till the very end, each story leaves you with a sense of place and time you will not easily forget as you ride along with the changing circumstances the characters brave, bluff and guess their way through.

Kate Casper, Editor

THE ZODIAC CLUB

his is the Riverside Dance Pavilion on Saturday night in April.

The river is running high yet, surging through willow brush along its bank out back. There in the light of a half moon, frogs were singing as I came in an hour ago. But I cannot hear the frogs now. From the next room instead, I hear *Smiling Joe and the Roustabouts* playing a polka on accordion, tuba, saxophone, and drums.

This hour already I have heard polkas three times, and each time I was thinking about my house up the county road a mile where Scorpio is sitting with my wife Ellen on my couch watching the ten o'clock news. They have just sent my kids to bed, and they are drinking a bottle of cherry-flavored vodka Scorpio has brought for my wife who prefers it. My dog sleeps at Scorpio's feet. Surely the stars are responsible for this.

I don't believe in astrology, but my wife is having an affair with Scorpio. His real name is Clark Everside, though around my house, I'm the only one who calls him that. Even both my kids call him Scorpio, their eyes widening and their small lips forming circles as they gush with the enthusiasm they have for comic-book heroes. Put Clark Everside's face on a small backpack, and they would trot off to school with it. My wife calls him Scorpio because he's a member of her astrology club, and they're all known to each other by their signs.

The *Zodiacs* they've named themselves—Crab, Capricorn, Scorpio, and a few others—but never more than one for each sign. So membership is limited, and if you happen to be a Scorpio yourself, forget it. You'll never get in as long as Clark is in, and of course with Clark in as far as he is, you will never believe my wife is the Virgin.

But I don't care. I'm not in the Zodiac Club. I have no designs of my own, neither in the sky nor in the future. My fingers on the bar just now are drumming a rhythm to the Roustabouts' latest polka. I don't believe my wife is the Virgin either, and I call her slick friend with his cherry vodka Clark Everside every chance I get because I hate the bastard.

High up, on a television at a corner of the bar, I can see the same ten o'clock news that's on my TV back home. If Smiling Joe were not playing next door, or if instead he were playing a slow, quiet waltz, I could even hear the news. But now I only see lips moving there in the glowing space above the sort of liquor bottles people only get into late at night when they're too drunk to think straight and into somebody's head pops a great idea for a nightcap with a name sounding like sex or violence. Above the sex and violence ingredients, lips move, but I hear nothing.

It suits me this way tonight because I myself feel that I have been failing to say something for a long time, moving my lips and making no sound. I have compassion for this talking head with his modeling-school smile, who wears a blue and white tie this evening of evenings, whose liquid delivery dries in the toots and squeaks of so much Roustabout rhythm. I have compassion for the frogs I can no longer hear.

A year ago, I wanted to say something foolish, something you've heard in a hundred second-rate films: "Clark Everside, get out of my house," I wanted to say. "Ellen, think of our babies."

There would have followed a scene with my wife collapsed in the stuffed flower-print chair in our living room. Later on would come an angry fit. She would say I had a dirty mind. She would run upstairs to pack her suitcase, shouting this over her shoulder for the neighbors to hear.

Out on the front lawn, Clark Everside would say in his calm, disgusting way, "You're making a big mistake, John. Better think it over." I'm glad I kept my mouth shut last year and avoided all that.

Why, in such times, are we all reduced to the melodramatic gestures of the silent movie? I could wave my arms and throw my hat on the ground. I could pull Clark Everside's nose and chase him through a hedge, while upstairs, both terror-stricken and flattered, my wife would watch from our bedroom window. Naturally the piano would be playing *presto*.

It wasn't supposed to be slapstick in my imagination, but if I'd spoken up a year ago, things would be much worse, I believe.

And so, I have come to this roadside bar in old-time movie fashion, the Roustabouts drowning out everything my drink hasn't gotten to yet, and once again, I want to say something that cannot be spoken. It was on my lips as I walked here this evening at sunset. "Clark Everside, go to hell," I meant to say. "Wife, I don't give a damn what you do anymore."

Theirs has not been one of those sneaky affairs, the sort portrayed in a song you've probably forgotten. "Slipping around, afraid we might be found," the song went. But Clark Everside has not been slipping around with my wife. He's been forthrightly out in the open with her in the living room of my house. He has the nonchalance of one who lives there.

He has not slunk out the back door as I came in the front. He has not climbed out our bedroom window while I showered. He comes in the front door, before and after me. My dog no longer barks at him, and he puts his coat in the hall closet without waiting for anyone to help him. Then he saunters into the kitchen to peer under steaming pot lids. "What's cooking?" he asks. He has even showered while I was in the bedroom.

"Ellen," I said, "why is our shower running, and who is that singing?"

"John," she replied, "it's Scorpio in our shower with his fine tenor. He helped me rake the leaves this afternoon when you were playing golf, and got so dirty. I couldn't send him home that way. What would his wife, poor Norma, think?"

I cannot answer such questions. I haven't seen Norma Everside for at least three months. She is a mousy, taciturn sort. Promise her a cleaning lady for life, and she would not tell you what she thinks of her husband in our shower at 5 o'clock in the afternoon.

Last year, I sometimes saw Norma with him at parties, and the more Clark Everside courted my wife, the mousier Norma became. She might have been pretty in the way the smallest cheerleader on your high school team was pretty, but Norma Everside took a turn toward mousy in her early thirties. The last time I saw her at a party, she seemed to inspect the wall by her chair for the nearest hole to occupy.

The television news is over. Meanwhile, above the whiskey bottles on a screen at the other end of the bar, we have the weather forecast. Everywhere else in here, we have Smiling Joe rollicking through another polka, the undercurrent of drumming feet on a dance floor. But now I am intent upon a system of charts and diagrams, a weatherman's sweeping gesture toward a low pressure center descending into the Great Plains.

Here is the new breed of weatherman to bring

us low pressure. Gone are the dull, gray men with thick glasses peering at the barometer and then prophesying. Instead, this sort wears a striped coat of the sort you might see on the deck of a cruise ship, his tie, a checkered affair. If I could hear him, he would have a joke for me tonight, and as toothy as he was, a few puns he thought funny. With the alacrity of a dancer, he slid across the floor from map to map.

Rain tomorrow in the Dakotas, by God, where they really need it, then tomorrow evening east and south upon our own heads where we could use a little too. It slashes across the moisture map as the glowing circle of depression swirls and chugs ahead, coiling downward like a flushing toilet. By this time tomorrow we all shall be whirling around in it, even as tonight we swing to Smiling Joe. Eastward I see blue high pressure sliding away through the Ohio Valley, pulling after it a pair of fronts like the pennant streamers fluttering over used car lots. High pressure is a breast spiraling upward to a nipple, ready by morning to clear the fog on our eastern seaboard.

I don't have a dirty mind. I am ready to speculate on the meaning of life, to set aside my narrow convictions, to seek harmony with universal rhythms. But tonight, as I see the weatherman's breast towering over Cincinnati, I can't help but think of my wife at this moment, with our television off now, the kids asleep, the dog confined to the study, and Clark Everside's hand under her blouse reaching from the Pennsylvania border to Muncie, Indiana and back again.

I believe they planned it this way when the Zodiacs convened at our house tonight. They knew I would leave after a while. I never stick around through a whole meeting. I go out for a walk and wind up here where I drink too much whenever the Zodiacs meet at our house with their ridiculous names and their talk of planets and constellations. My wife and Clark Everside don't have to sneak around. They just invite their strange friends to my house. They start talking about the heavens, and I run away.

I could have upset their plans by staying home tonight, and to give them a scare, I even made a show of it. When their meeting was about to begin, I went to the hall closet with Capricorn's jacket and then returned to the living room without my own. My wife, on the couch between Leo and the Crab, glanced at Scorpio in the flower-print chair.

"I'll be in the basement workshop if you want anything," I said.

The Virgin stiffened, Scorpio smiled, and Capricorn, a well-formed goat in her early twenties, wiggled around in a card-table chair. "You're so kind to all of us," she said, showing me a better pair of legs than you'll usually find on a goat.

In my basement, a sheet of plywood waited to become a doghouse. I took out my carpenter's pencil and went to work on it, drawing rectangular sides and triangles to form its gable. I fit my pattern carefully onto the plywood sheet, once erasing an entire triangle to make better use of the sheet. Finally I eased the sheet onto my saw table. Music, muffled and distant, descended on me.

The Zodiacs always adorn their meeting with a sort of anthem, one of them recorded from the soundtrack of an old science fiction film. Even coming through the floor and two insulated walls, it sounded starry. I flipped the switch on my saw and lingered for a moment over the precise landscape of my plywood drawings—a schematic of rectangles and triangles where I imagined the Virgin, Scorpio, and myself in the corners. Who really gave a damn anyway? Not even the dog.

I cut the whole thing straight down the middle. When my saw ripped through to the other end, I had two pieces the same size. My triangles were trapezoids.

I could still hear the starry music, so again I flipped the switch and drove my whirling blade through two thicknesses. Another burst of saw-dust, a last elephantine scream, and I had four pieces the same size. Again I cut at these.

My dog house shrank to something you might hang from a tree for lovebirds. Then I had pieces for bookends. Halving these, I created doorstops. From other pieces came laths to stake out a veg-etable garden, paddles to stir paint, wedges to balance a wobbly desk. I was on my way to swizzle sticks when I cut my thumb and gave up.

The sawdust was atmospheric, an ochre haze settling on the broken homes of dog and bird and man, and I had been choking for some time without really thinking about it. Yellow mounds lay on the floor along the perimeter of my saw table, a drifted peak in the near corner. My shirt and pants were awash with it. My hair was sprin-kled with gold.

I turned off the saw and went back upstairs, looking like a madman, I'm sure, as I strolled through the living room with my bleeding thumb wrapped in a handkerchief.

The music had stopped, and my wife was

reading to the members next month's forecast from an astrology consulting service. She paused. For an instant I was fixed in the gaze of heavenly creatures—a goat, a crab, a lion, a fish, a scorpion. I swept by them on my way to the bathroom. Behind me, on our dark living-room carpet, lay a trail of sawdust footprints.

Leaving the door ajar, I bandaged my thumb, took off my shirt and shook sawdust from its pocket, washed sawdust from my neck, combed it from my hair, emptied my shoes, and eavesdropped on the meeting.

My wife finished her reading with a perceptible tremble in her voice. Then Capricorn reported on a new book by an astrologer who recast horoscopes according to the positions of a minor asteroid that might collide with the earth in several million years.

"We should all read this and discuss it next meeting," Capricorn suggested earnestly. I recall thinking that she had a smooth, soft voice to go with her good legs.

"It's just a fad," said my wife. "These things come and go."

"No, it's not," said Capricorn. "It changes everything for all of us. Our lives aren't what we thought."

I heard Leo clear his throat. He was a thin insect of a man who nursed a tremor and more nearly resembled a praying mantis than a lion. "I always figured something was wrong," he said.

"Right or wrong," the Crab said, "it's all too complicated for me."

"It's hard enough to keep up with the planets," Scorpio said. "Now there's something out there we can't see and never heard of before. Who wants to keep track of that?"

I knew my wife would be nodding, the Crab would agree, and over by the fireplace, the Fish was chewing gum and agreeing. Leo cleared his throat again but said nothing. Capricorn would lose this one, partly because my wife envied her legs. They wouldn't read her book. To hell with asteroids.

"But," I heard Capricorn say, and I kicked the door shut with my foot.

I was dizzy again with this talk of stars, the endless discussions of opposition and conjunction, rocks toiling through space, animals dancing with planets, dodging in and out of the light as the earth ran its course. I left the bathroom with sawdust in a wet ring around the sink, with a mound on the floor by the bathtub. I hurried out the back door, away from the stars.

Crab, you are right, I now add upon reflection. It's also too complicated for me. I abhor these constellations more than the doghouse patterns on my plywood sheet with their false promise of comforts beyond reach. With my saw a'whirling through the universe, I would cut them down to their individual stars.

Once again, Capricorn, you are also right, for the heavens have changed us. None of us are what we thought because of things we cannot see, and tomorrow when the sun rises again, no matter what we remember or forget, the stars will keep on dancing out of sight and tell half the story or maybe none.

On television, we have the sports now on both the screens I can see from my barstool. It began with a montage of film clips—a sports car running off the road at Les Mans, a jump shot from seventeen feet, a bass dancing over the still, turquoise waters of the Upper Forge, a runner sliding into second, and as the swirling dust settles, a cheerleader doing the splits. Our announcer is a great fat man in a peach-colored sports coat, two sizes too small and bursting open, oyster fashion, at the lapels as he leans forward to report a shutout in Pittsburgh. This I can even hear, for the night has moved along to the fabled witching hour, and Smiling Joe has grown maudlin in the next room.

At my house, Clark Everside has gone to the recreation room with my wife. It is up over the garage with a blue and green carpet in the pattern of a stained-glass window, a pool table in the center, an old television and studio couch from our apartment days, and a lock on the door left over from the previous owner who rented it out as a room to help pay a mortgage he couldn't pay anyway.

I will now leave my stool at the bar because I'm afraid the great fat man in his peach coat will show instant replays from the room over my garage. Of course, this is absurd.

I am neither crazy, nor drunk, but I don't want to see Clark Everside on the couch with my wife in slow motion. I don't want to be tricked into witnessing this, and though the fat man may laugh till his jowls flap as he describes it, though he may say that's the way the old ball bounces, it's a sad and dreary truism to describe Clark Everside in action six feet above my wife's Volkswagen.

"Well, better luck next time," the sportscaster says. He bursts through his lapels once more as laughter ripples through his wobbling chin. "The game is over when the last man is out," he adds, while I walk to the garlanded entrance of the dance pavilion.

The dance floor is open on its river side, screened along that wall and overhead. Booths line the other wall as far as its roof extends toward the river. Most of these are empty at the moment as the floor is cluttered with dancers.

The Roustabouts play on an elevated platform with their backs to the screen and the river. They wear red blazers and white pants. Their faces are red. The accordionist is leading them into a slow waltz. From his knees, he sways gently with its rhythm.

The dancers spin and glide past me. Among them, another vision haunts me: Norma Everside with her head resting on the shoulder of a man who is not Clark Everside. Our eyes meet for a moment in the pavilion gloaming. She does not raise her head, but looks out rather as a mouse from the security of its cranny. Her eyes are crystal. In them leap microscopically the flames of a dozen gaslights flickering along the pavilion walls. She whirls by and evaporates into the throng. The Roustabouts' last waltzing note falls upon Smiling Joe's drum, temporizes there, and then springs skyward while a hundred dancers recalibrate. Smiling Joe has yet another polka for this evening.

I return to my stool at the bar where both television screens are blank, a sign of the end approaching, and where a woman I know two stools away stares into the bar mirror at me. Capricorn smiles as I recognize her. She too has come down the country road along the river from my house. In front of her, a vodka gimlet glows iridescent in the bar lights.

"Capricorn," I imagine myself saying, breathing my thoughts toward her reflection, "Who am I, Capricorn? Guess, if you can?"

"You, John, are Libra," I can hear her saying, "and now that I have told you what you wanted, sit here and drink beside me, and soon we will dance the last waltz next door."

Here is a fantasy to linger upon. I see Capricorn with me in the pavilion with the other dancers on its perimeter enclosing us in a great circle. We waltz around in it. Smiling Joe, suddenly with flowing white hair and wearing now a red tuxedo, directs what has become the philharmonic. Capricorn has exchanged her red skirt for a long white ball gown, and as I sweep her over the polished floor in broad graceful arcs, I hear the comforting rustle of crinoline and whalebone stay. I have become a magnificent dancer. Then I hear Capricorn's voice from two stools away, and my dream music stops.

"Didn't it work out for you tonight?" she asks.

"What?" I ask into the mirror.

"Whatever you were making with your saw in the basement. We couldn't hear each other upstairs for a half hour." She laughs as if she didn't care to hear the others anyway. In the mirror I can see her small white teeth.

"I was making swizzle sticks, but I cut myself and gave up at the doorstop stage." I raise my bandaged thumb so she can see it in the mirror.

"Swizzle sticks—I wouldn't have guessed that." She pauses to sip her drink. "How do you make swizzle sticks?"

"Start with an eight-foot sheet of plywood when you don't want to build a doghouse," I say. "It's tricky—you can wind up with toothpicks if you're not careful."

Capricorn sips her drink bemused, and I am ready to describe for her the whole artsy business of swizzle stick construction, to explain that my old retriever licks the hand of Clark Everside, forfeiting his new house, but Capricorn, perhaps sensing a dissertation, asks no more about it. She plays with her drink instead, and, in the bar mirror, studies me over the brim of her glass.

Perhaps she thinks I'm crazy, and she is looking for a maniacal twitch at the corners of my mouth. I order another whiskey and stare back. Even above the legs, Capricorn is not a bad looking woman. In her eyes I dare to believe is the gleaming promise of friendship. Behind us flanking the pavilion door, two gaslights flicker and reflect in the bar mirror. I wonder if this instead is what I perceive in Capricorn's eyes, but I dream anyway because here is the warm, scintillating stuff of fantasy.

I want to speak to her again, but Smiling Joe has grown very loud for a quarter past midnight, and she would have to shout. Feet are drumming on the dance floor again, the whole place shakes, so how can Capricorn shout above this din to say she wants me sitting closer, buying her a drink, dancing the last waltz? Yet this is what I see in her eyes, so I keep staring into the mirror and dreaming.

What an advantage is a mirror for such blatant flirtations. Were we doing this across a room from each other, people would stop talking and wait for something either sexual or violent to happen, but it is only glass we watch. No more than an image on a wall is Capricorn. I may safely gaze and dream awhile. My whiskey comes, and I push three dollars across the bar.

"And two bits," the bartender says.

I snag a quarter from what was meant to be his tip. I dream until a ring of car keys slides down to me from Capricorn's hand. I catch them and scramble over the two bar stools between us.

"What's this?" I ask foolishly, bending near her so I don't have to shout. I am so close I can smell rose fragrances in her hair. She cannot hear above the polka, she says by pointing to her ear, a small delicious ear for a goat. I put my lips there and say only a bit more loudly. "What am I supposed to do with your keys?" A small pearl is hanging from her lobe by a golden ring, and I am close enough to lick it if I want. And I want to catch that pearl in my teeth, swimming upward with it to the surface of an azure pool where a friend waits in a boat to accept my treasure.

"Would you go to my car for me," she asks, "and toss this cell phone in the glove box?" She pulls her phone from a coat pocket. "I won 't be needing it here, I'm sure."

Won't be needing it here, I'm sure. I break the surface of the azure pool, shaking the water from my face and sucking the short, spasmodic breaths of a man nearly drowned.

"The green Infinity by the river with a stuffed tiger in the back window. When you get back, we can dance if you like."

Green Infinity and a stuffed tiger, by God! We can dance, by God! I rush outside and down to the riverbank where a line of cars is parked. The half-moon has set now, and the sky has become a dark, star-filled vaulting spread above the willow trees.

I find the Infinity with a tiger in it. I get rid of the cell phone, and I linger for a moment to think about what's happening.

Overhead I see more than stars. I see the shapes of familiar things I wanted to obliterate just minutes ago—a virgin, a lion in the western treetops, the head of a scorpion near the horizon where the three red lights of a transmission tower blink with random nonchalance. I am Libra, and I'm up there with them where we are all moving as we always have, night and day, in the sky and in the river where their starlight shimmers on nights grown as black as this was until just a moment ago.

It is a harmony I hear as well in the singing frogs breeding among the willow brush nearby. I could find it now behind me in the pavilion where Norma Everside twirls among the drumming feet. We share this rhythm with the stars and with the river. We dance in the sky and on the polished floor, holding hands. We whirl in a great circle, and we sing with the frogs. The song must outlast even Smiling Joe who will play this night in the pavilion a last waltz for Capricorn and me.

A FURTHER REPORT ON
COMET KAHOUTEK

*P*inecrest Observatory was neither large nor well known, even in its part of the country where telescopes are not found on every good hilltop. It was an anachronistic appendage, an eccentric charitable bequeathment of the Gibley Foundation whose money originated in creosoted railroad ties and then flourished in crushed rock and on-site-mixed concrete.

Allan Clive, its only director and lone astronomer-in-residence from 1955 till the early seventies, was better known, especially on both coasts where there is a greater interest in popular scientific literature. That said, few people within five hundred miles of Pinecrest would have known Clive at all prior to the appearance of

Comet Kahoutek. A man of solitary habits, he liked it that way. Privacy was a bit of good luck he hardly expected. Being a scientific writer had afforded him some reluctant fame, so he was happy for the opportunity of true solitude.

One of the second-generation Gibley men built Pinecrest and its adjoining residence to pursue his stargazing hobby. He used Gibley concrete, impossible to get for most projects in the aftermath of World War Two. Gibley crushed rock lined its circular drive. Its service roads wound through groves of virgin timber, lone survivors of the family railroad tie boom days a half century before.

Pinecrest's astronomical hardware, an old thirty-six inch Von Leyden refractor, brass-mounted, with photographic and spectroscopic accessories, cost half a million at the time and couldn't be found today for a Gibley's ransom. Purchased from a Belgium university, the telescope is the only one of its kind in North America. Today, aside from being of antiquarian interest, this adds little to the observatory's reputation.

The stargazing Gibley was either Vincent or Jimmy. Local curiosity once swirled around this question, in as much as the Gibley's are pinewoods equivalents of *beautiful people*. One of these men—some say both—kept a mistress in the observatory residence. This may explain the sudden abandonment of Pinecrest. The divorces of both Vincent and Jimmy led to the disgrace of the Gibley dynasty in the late forties.

Later, their mother Julia Gibley used the residence for two seasons as a summer house, but the observatory itself was left empty nearly a decade before another second-generation Gibley gave it all away for tax reasons to the only school within a hundred miles, stipulating as well, an annual sum to staff the place. The state forestry college eagerly accepted this gift, though its president let out privately at the time that the property's remaining stands of virgin white pine were his only interest. More privately yet, he joked that those trees were about the only virgins up there, from what he heard.

One way to drive *up there* from the forestry college is east and then north through the Huffton Lakes region whose many resorts are famous for picture postcards and July festival pike fries. This route veers briefly northwest on a county tar road. The turn is well marked by Tandy Corners Grocery, a gas station and 3.2 beer tavern with a milk cooler and bread rack.

You approach the observatory ground from the southeast. The building itself cannot be viewed favorably from this direction, owing to the hilly terrain, but its service road is identified both by a college sign and an overturned six-foot drainage tile which Julia Gibley adapted as a geranium planter.

Allan Clive preferred to drive another way: west from the forestry college on the Interstate—formerly the old military highway—and then north on the Splays Creek Road—tar all the way until it cuts east where the last six miles are good gravel, mostly Gibley. This is a route for the solitude-minded, the lover of nature, the man with a good car. No gas stations and taverns mar the scene, not so much as a cabin the last thirty miles, and on Gibley gravel, the road becomes one lane, winding through splendid woodland marshes, cedar and tamarack on the verge, heron rookeries, arrowhead lush in the watery ditches, and sometimes a moose on the road. At the end of this is a fine view of the observatory on a distant hill in its pine-tree clearing, an aesthetic advantage that seemed to weigh most heavily upon Allan Clive's navigation. He genuinely loved Pinecrest, and one of his life's greatest pains was his conviction that it would never amount to beans astronomically.

Clive was of that scientific breed who couldn't make it in the classroom, and since the forestry college offered no astronomy courses, he was left alone with Gibley money to write and do what research he could on Baron von Leyden's hand-crafted masterpiece, the limitations of which he was most willing to accept in exchange for privacy, solitude, and reprieve from the lecture audiences he feared to the point of hysteria.

Given time, he always insisted privately—staving off the despair to which he was especially prone in later years—he would learn to control this fear of the live audience. It was a child's fear with him, old as the black bears he no longer feared, peering in at his darkened window screen.

He could remember a grade-school nun reassuring him about this before a Christmas play. "Just think of all those people as cabbages in a garden," the nun had said.

He thought of this on those occasions he could not avoid speaking somewhere, but like so much advice one could never forget, it wasn't worth a damn, not even at the time. Much better it was to stay among the virgin pines, polishing the old brass hardware of Gibley self-indulgence. He had books to write and articles, both for scientific journals and the popular magazines. His professional articles included "Class C Variable in Scorpio" and "The Potassium-Sodium Contents of Globular Members." His best-known popular article was probably "The Comet as Cosmic Carpet Sweeper," published nationally the summer before Kahoutek appeared.

Someday, he hoped to face the crowd and speak in the easy manner of his writing style. His legs would not tremble nor his voice flail the air searching for words that had slipped from view and suddenly become impossible sounds no one could pronounce. Given time, he hoped, this fear might go the way of one's black bears, an extinct species of the personal zoo. There are some problems that only the clock's ticking will solve. One must wait, and so he waited, shuddering his way through the few cabbage patches he could not gingerly avoid from his Pinecrest solitude.

Clive was a bachelor. He lived alone in the observatory residence, refurnishing it with his own money and restoring both of Julia Gibley's wildflower rock gardens. Her yellow lady slippers he rescued in their eleventh hour from an invasion of sneezeweed. He had few visitors, and his phone seldom rang. Once a year he dined with the Gibley Foundation directors at a formal meeting where all beneficiaries of Gibley wealth presented annual reports and expressions of gratitude. His relationship with the forestry college was even more tenuous.

He was listed a faculty member in the 1957-59 college bulletin but unaccountably dropped from sight after that. Spring and autumn, busloads of forestry students searched the observatory ground for plant specimens, insects, and suspicious fungi. To some of these he had once been introduced as the *Chief Forester*, a designation he accepted as a joke, never learning that around the college it was **the** joke in those days when the president, a vulgar man among his fellows, had called Pinecrest Observatory the school's "third tit." After a while, that particular president died, the jokes died, and even Allan Clive's name died, lapsing into a local obscurity best compared to Comet Kahoutek in deep space before a teasing gravitational gesture nudged it toward the sun.

In Clive's case, the nudge—altering forcefields of mass and matter—was the dedication of a new forestry college campus the very week Kahoutek was predicted to be its brightest. V. G. Parnell, nicknamed "Very Good," was college publicity director and dedication program chairman. He had discovered Clive's name while paging through the 1957-59 college bulletin searching for what he thought of as historical background. In his mind at the time was a dedication program which had students costumed as trees reenacting in pageant form the school's history. To his wife over a supper of mashed potatoes, peas, and walleyed pike the day he discovered Clive, he said something like, "Jesus Christ. Imagine, an astronomer at this tree college, and nobody I talk to has ever so much as seen him." A few days later, he read about Kahoutek, "Comet of the Century." He found Clive's article on the cosmic carpet sweeper and forgot all about students dressed as trees.

Something would happen that had never happened before, and perhaps not for a hundred thousand years, if ever, would Kahoutek come again with its light bright enough to be seen even by day. "Very Good" Parnell saw his whole dedication program in cometary light. He saw a tidy raise for himself forming in its tail. The college band, green clad as medieval foresters, would play the national anthem, a local clergyman give the invocation, and the college president speak about forestry and the college's future on its new campus. Then Clive would come forward to introduce the comet. With the band playing a peppy recessional, the astronomer would lead three thousand or so guests outside into the January twilight where Kahoutek would bloom, its tail—Parnell had read—possibly in a six-part fan extending to the zenith.

It was late October, and in Julia Gibley's restored rock gardens, bottle gentians were blooming among the dried and frost-bitten remains of weaker plants. Allan Clive refused Parnell's invitation to be a dedication speaker. In November, with greater trepidation, he refused the college president's invitation. Word next came from the Gibley Foundation. Parnell had appealed to them. A foot of snow covered the observatory grounds, and among professional astronomers, Kahoutek was already a worry, nearly two full magnitudes fainter than predictions.

Over the phone with "Very Good" Parnell, Clive had tried to explain this, but Parnell couldn't understand. "All the papers say it'll be a big one. Don't worry," he said. "We want to print the dedication programs. How about it?" His tone was threatening. The Gibley Foundation letter had been threatening. Clive gave in.

"Comets," he had begun a popular article,

"ages ago were portents of disaster and harbingers of doom."

He could not imagine an audience of three thousand cabbages in the forestry college fieldhouse. He stammered and lost his way. He drooled and shook. He had wanted to explain in simple terms how comets were very unpredictable, especially those like Kahoutek that had possibly never visited the sun before. One could not know what might happen to such a comet's tail. Kahoutek was now dimmer by a thousand times than anyone had at first expected, but it was still breathtaking in the subtle way of the best wildflowers, he wanted to say. His own breath was taken away, however, and he couldn't say any of it. He froze to the stage like a corpse in the snow.

Parnell himself led the audience outside, never believing until that very moment that the comet wouldn't be there. Some people thought they saw something, but generally, everybody was laughing, their breath throwing up clouds of steam as they stomped around in the cold to keep their feet warm.

Parnell and the college president proved to be humorless men. They somehow blamed Clive, whose actions on the stage indicated guilt, they thought. The Gibley Foundation officers were equally embarrassed since most of them were present, and the forestry college had widely publicized their gift of the observatory and its astronomer.

Clive returned to Pinecrest and stayed on for a few months.

In May of 1974, he was informed that the forestry college and the Gibley Foundation had renegotiated its bequeathment so that the observatory and its residence would become a camp for college foresters. The Von Leyden refractor was dismantled and stored beneath the college gymnasium. Julia Gibley's rock gardens have sneezeweed again. Allan Clive moved out west somewhere and hasn't been heard from in these parts. Kahoutek, scientists now predict, will return in a quarter of a million years.

SEVEN YEARS WITH
URANUS IN SCORPIO

*D*elores and Paul were once in love, but now that has gone down the drain. So it goes with so many stars floating around in the universe: Lisa and Frank, Beth and Rick ... or was that Rick and Tracy? It all becomes hazy.

Delores believed in astrology. She ran to her friends with predictions, and if they weren't home, she left strips of them—cut from books—taped to their doors and apartment mailboxes. With her mobile phone, she sent them text messages. Every year she bought forecasts for the twelve months to come, sun signs and moon. She knew the chances for illness and financial success, the rewards and perils of friendship and love. *Beware of the stock market in July,* she once warned her mother, who owned no stocks and thought Wall Street a sort of dike keeping the North Atlantic out of Manhattan.

You may meet this autumn an Aries who will change your life.

In October Delores met Paul who wasn't an Aries, but a tail-end Fish. For Delores this was close enough. Two days before Christmas, she read the last page of the year's forecast. It was bad luck, she thought, to read far ahead.

Next month, Uranus will enter the sign of Scorpio. For seven years personal relationships will be stormy and confused. Avoid all entanglements.

She read this to Paul as they sat together in her living room the same evening. He threw her book in the fireplace.

"Screw your astrology," he said in a voice spongy with love and apple brandies.

Delores might have retrieved her book. The fire wasn't big, a single artificial log flickering red and green flames, and Paul's aim was bad. She had time while it smoldered to one side of the grate, but she stayed at Paul's side, his woman now, no matter what Uranus did. "The year is almost over, anyway," she said with a sigh.

A month later, they became engaged up in the mountains in a shabby, ski-town bar called Casmey's. Paul's work colleague Tracy and her beau Rick tagged along, looking forward to the prospect of an unpredictable night out.

Casmey's wasn't on the main trail of the southern California crowds. It wasn't an establishment with bigger plans than burning down with its insurance paid up and staving off bankruptcy meantime. For years its customers had been mostly people who got lost and didn't know how they came there, and then got drunk and didn't know how they left. Every Saturday night of the winter they heard the same five-piece band —a local Sierra group—that sweated a lot, drank a lot between sets, used each other's first names a lot, and worked the audience a lot with ploys like, *"Didn't Glen do a great job with that last number, folks? And now let's give our drummer Kevin a big hand!"*

But nothing makes sense in California—how things catch on and how they don't. Casmey's incredible inferiority had become its great attraction, and out of the blue, from trying to save money and cut every corner, old man Casmey's cash drawers were rupturing, and he was having a tough time managing his crowds. For the first time in his life, he hired bouncers, two windburnt, burley guys resembling chainsaw sculptures in ski sweaters and stocking caps, flanking his entrance with their arms folded.

Paul suggested stopping for the same reason everyone stopped, so they could all say they heard the best worst band around and drank the best worst drinks.

"Telling stories afterwards is half the fun," giggled Tracy. She winked at Delores. They both figured on having plenty to tell after this trip.

Casmey's drinks were long on mix and short on what counted. His food was the sort that shuts down truck stops. Nobody complained. The cool ambience of this down-and-out dive was what they came for. It was, after all, the scene to be seen in, reality TV in ski country. Old Casmey himself stood at the door looking like a high school principal who'd become suddenly iconic. He was also twice the age of anyone else there, gray-haired with dark brows that might have been mustaches for Hitler costumes.

He was surprised to be a millionaire and folk hero when doing these same things most of his life had nearly ruined him. He wore the same salmon-colored jacket he had worn as a failure, with shoulders so padded he seemed to be sprouting wings. He wore the same broken-down loafers, the same gabardine pants, shiny in the knees and seat. He didn't want to change his act and ruin the gimmick, whatever it was. He was afraid to change his underwear. Instead of praying for a fire, he thought of updating his sprinkler system.

He waved a flashlight in one hand and a rubber stamp in the other to ink the wrists of those who paid his cover charge coming in. Where people had once hated this, it was now praised as the ultimate tackiness. They used to swear when he stamped their wrists, but now they swore if he didn't stamp both. After a while, when it got hot out on the dance floor, Casmey's red ink ran down to their fingers and smeared on their faces when they brushed delirium from their eyes. They awoke in the morning looking like Christ in a passion play.

Later in the evening, Paul gave Delores a full carat solitaire, lightly tinted green and set in platinum. She was drunk and mounted a table to see it better near a yellow ceiling light.

"You ought to have a look up here," she squealed down to Tracy. Tracy climbed up on her chair.

The band began a striptease tune while Delores reeled on the table, twisting her ring to display its facets. Rick leaned forward and peered up her skirt like a goat eyeing an apple bush.

"Hubba! Hubba!" he sang out.

Paul wasn't amused. In the fight that followed, Delores tumbled off the table with eyes glistening to match her diamond.

Casmey ducked behind the bar and called the police. His chainsaw sculptures came charging through the front entrance. Since brawls were a part of his act, Casmey didn't mind. He just had to appear to mind.

Tracy put an arm around Delores to back her away from the fray. "They're only horsing around," she said as Paul ripped the pocket from Rick's coat. "Paul is so old-fashioned. It comes from growing up in Iowa, but it's a lovely ring, honey, and he's a hunk. Don't cry on a night like this."

The next morning, Delores and Tracy met Paul and Rick at the jail. They came out like old friends rescued from a shipwreck, arms around each other, singing through a day's growth of beard, wearing the clothes they'd slept in.

Delores flourished her ring in the brilliant sunlight of a Sunday morning whose new snow covered the lawn and shrubbery outside the jail. Snow crystals flashed and glinted.

"The world is so full of diamonds," Delores cooed, clutching Tracy's hand.

"What did I tell you?" Tracy said. "They were horsing around."

Delores kissed Paul. Tracy kissed Rick. Rick kissed Delores, and Paul kissed Tracy. They danced together down the street to Tracy's apple-green SUV with four pairs of skis in a rack on top. Not even a new parking ticket under the windshield wiper could spoil their fun. Tracy stuffed it behind the elastic waistband of her ski pants.

"Want help with that?" asked Rick with a smirk.

"Later," said Tracy.

The mountains in winter sunlight were purple and blue, but now all that's gone down the drain....

The year Rick met Beth, and Tracy hooked up with Tom, Paul and Delores moved into a run-down little tract house realtors had advertised as a bungalow with possibilities.

As soon as Paul had driven off to his job for an Anaheim loan company their first morning there, Delores went shopping for paint. Her ring flashing under the hardware store lights suddenly seemed to be a cruel anachronism and betrayal.

Paul had lied. He turned out to be poorer and with fewer prospects than he let on before they were married. He'd spent most of his savings on the ring. They were years away from a decent house with real possibilities.

Her own family had paid off the mortgage before she was born on what seemed a mansion compared to this. She had grown up on maple floors, carpeted staircases, three toilets, and a swimming pool. It hadn't seemed at the time all that much to brag about, but like many children of spacious homes and six-digit parent incomes, she had silly notions of economy. Frugality had seemed as mythological as a unicorn, as outlandish as a platypus.

Now frugality lay in wait as sure as cold raw meat on a swollen eye from Paul's most recent barroom brawl. Frugality meant buying, on sale, eight gallons of a paint called *Blushing Peach* for a one-gallon living room, a two-quart kitchen and bedroom, an eggcup bath, and a husband who despised blushing peach, even on peaches.

They fought, and Paul shoved her, one of those half-serious, mostly symbolic, Iowa farmboy gestures that in another context might have been seen as happy-go-lucky.

"If only you'd accept help from my parents,"

Delores sobbed. He pushed her backward to their bedroom door where she banged her head once, then several times as a lunatic would. She locked herself in and cried herself to sleep while Paul stayed up with a bottle of bourbon.

At midnight, he got into the paint cans, and then he broke down the bedroom door. Since it wasn't much of a door, it snapped open with but one solid run at it, leaving Delores little time to be startled before she found herself in Paul's amorous embrace.

Not long after, the first shadows of dawn were forming in their narrow backyard. A garbage truck labored down the alley. A sparrow chirped. Late evening flights from the East Coast descended through a haze. Paul left for work, leaving Delores in a haze of her own, pondering her discovery that sex could be better after a fight.

An hour later, she stirred from her reverie, and lifting her head from the pillow, saw the blushing peach living room walls through her broken bedroom door. Her kitchen was also blushing peach—walls and trim, cupboards, refrigerator, sink, and doorknobs. Everything in the house was blushing peach, down to the bathtub and their one flush toilet.

"He's just a tail-end Fish," said Delores.

Delores bought more paint with a hundred her father slipped her. She tried to cover the blushing peach in her house, but what is harder to conceal than a blush? White turned pink, powder blue went mauve, green turned orange, her toilet to the color of rouge on an old woman's cheek.

Paul took up bowling and erotic thoughts. He stayed out late most nights, claiming to be at work or stuck in traffic, and at last not bothering to claim anything. He dreamt of other women he had loved, going back as far as a waitress in Keokuk. When that seemed too far, he thought about Tracy.

Louise and Sam bowled one evening in the lane two over from his. He watched Louise throwing her lithe body into that heavy black ball, somehow sweeping it gracefully away to the pins which danced in circles and fell before her, bringing down others with them. He bought Sam a beer and moved to their lane for the next game. When she left four standing in the tenth frame, he threw his ball among her pins. He never bowled better, winning five dollars from Sam, though Louise beat them both with her two strikes and six at the end.

At home, Delores studied her toilet, still blushing months later under two fresh coats of enamel. Reading in the indelibility of blushing peach the intransigence of all old passions, for the first time since her engagement, she thought of Rick.

Tracy also thought of Rick, and Louise must have been thinking of Paul as she flexed her hips toward him on the lane. Further out in the universe, there were other pairings going awry as Verna thought of Tom, and Lisa thought of Richard, and Barbara also thought of Paul. Constance thought of Frank, and Lisa thought of Todd, and Beth thought of Phil, and Inez thought of Sam. Nothing was real. It was worse than being alone.

When Paul came home from bowling, Delores showed him the blushing toilet.

"It's just right," he said. "If you were a toilet, wouldn't you blush a little?" He studied Delores with his ice-blue eyes, and she blushed like the toilet for thinking of Rick.

"It's hard to paint over," she said. "It's so smooth, the new paint keeps sliding off the old."

Life was a lot like that.

Together in bed that night, Paul tried to imagine he was with Louise instead. Delores tried to imagine Rick. Rick imagined Tracy whom, after all, he'd known before Beth. Richard imagined Constance. Phil imagined Verna. And on it went.

Next morning, after Paul left for work, Delores cleaned her paint brushes and put them in a coffee can under the kitchen sink. She poured a pint of thinner into the can. She figured she was done painting for a while.

From his loan company office, Paul called Sam to invite him out to lunch. Their chat at the bowling alley had revealed that Sam needed money, so over a third cup of coffee, they got around to discussing a loan through Paul's company, an "insider's" loan as Paul described it. Sam would get low interest, easy terms, no questions. Paul would get Louise.

"Confidentially," Sam added as he signed a contract the same afternoon in Paul's office, "I see Inez now and then, and she thinks there's a kid coming."

So Sam needed money to pay for Inez's abortion, and when Louise found out, she and Sam went down the drain. Paul cut in without complaint from Sam who needed more money to pay his attorney, and since Paul didn't make him wait, he didn't make Paul wait. Delores found out from

Rick. Barbara found out about Phil from Tom. Verna found out from Todd, and Lisa from Richard, and Tracy from Phil. So all these tenuous pairings went down the drain.

In a strip mall where Delores now runs a boutique, a jeweler buys used stuff—rings and love tokens by the score—which he sends out of town like used cars with too many miles on them for the wise local trade. Beth swears she saw Delores' green solitaire on a finger in Reno at the slot next over when she spent a week there with Tom. And Richard went somewhere with Constance—and so on. But now, all this has gone down the drain.

During the seven years Uranus spent in Scorpio, Delores lost a lot of sleep listening to tales like these, telling her own about her marriages and relationships, trying to see shapes matching those and the stars. After her last heavy-duty, stellar breakup, she ate out a lot, was taken to concerts and football games and once to a water show of dolphins playing polo. Everyone thought she must be lonely, with too much time on her hands and too few men in her life, so they invited her to everything and introduced her all around and left her with barely time to run her boutique.

She met a dozen recently-divorced or otherwise unattached, disconnected men resembling failed lounge lizard musicians. They might have all been brothers. They had always just come driving in from Reno or Tahoe or up north somewhere, or were about to drive up to Reno or Tahoe or up north somewhere. Swarthy sorts, most of them, tanned and toothy, in colorful jackets and dark, open shirts, the kind of worn-out losers who sit alone at a bar lying to themselves if there's nobody else to lie to. They turn their heads every time a door opens to see if it's somebody they know. It's never anybody they know.

They all had stories. Everyone in California had stories. Sometimes you thought this the main point of doing things: so you'd have stories to tell. Their plots and characters intersected and criss-crossed and seemed to Delores like the refrain of a song for a game like cakewalk. It was all too stupid for words. Only an astrologer could make any sense out of it.

Louise and Frank installed a new toilet in Delores and Rick's old love nest. "What kind of a moron tries painting a toilet?" Louise asked.

"The world is full of them," said Frank, with his arm around her waist, and then in a burst of passion, he added, "Baby, I just know we're going to make this work."

At first, since they both stood there looking at it, she thought he meant their new toilet.

Monday last week, Tracy bounced into Delores' boutique.

"I'm still horsing around, but I'm getting a little tired of it," Tracy said.

"I'm not surprised," said Delores, straightening a display of silks hung from silver rings, letting them slide through her fingers. "I just read in my astrology forecast that Uranus is finally on the move."

Somewhere nearby was a black hole, a cosmic drain, something so heavy that all the stars were sucked into it and never came out.

WORKMAN AT LATHE

iving off the record was what I called living with Maryann. I had reached that time in my life where I seemed to drift beyond records—beyond a certificate of birth and a parish record of my baptism, beyond the death certificates of both my parents—deceased in Minnesota at either end of the decade past—and beyond my marriage license and divorce decree, filed in Michigan at opposite ends of a year recently past. With Maryann, no records were kept, and I thought I was in a stage of my life where there would be none.

We had not so much as a parking ticket in common for the nearly two years we lived together. We rented our second-floor front apartment in her name and bought a car in mine. We were never in the same credit bureau file. I bought the newspaper, and her name was on the mailbox in the entryway downstairs. I remember waiting for the postman the day after we moved in.

"Also for Jack Muller," I said to him pointing to the fresh white card in our mailbox's name slot. There was Maryann's name neatly typed.

"Also for Jack Muller," he repeated in the monotone of a school boy memorizing names of the Presidents. "Okay," he said, "it complicates things if you leave your name off the box, but I'll try to remember. How long is it going to be *also for Jack Muller?*"

"It's permanent," I said.

"Okay," he said.

I sensed he was making an effort not to smile. He began sorting mail into the other apartment boxes. I heard him whistling as I walked back upstairs.

What was complicated for him that morning was simpler for me the day it proved not to be *permanently also for Jack Muller.* Maryann and I had polished off our romance and found tedium beneath its glitter. I was happy there were no forms to fill out the early spring morning of west wind and snow squalls I left her sleeping on our hide-a-bed.

The inevitability of our separation had been clear to both of us for months as far back as when the cottonwood outside our apartment still had its leaves. Jittery kingbirds were still churning out new broods which seemed an affront to our already diminished capacities for each other.

With the cottonwood turning yellow, Maryann began complaining of a heart murmur, a condition for which there was scant medical evidence and which I regarded as metaphorical only. What murmured in Maryann's heart—with leaves carpeting the boulevard—was the feeling that we should part.

We both saw it coming in our routine of daily spats followed by intervals of silence which offered more a chance to rest than any resolution. My only surprise, when the end finally came, was in leaving her warm side and tumbling so competently into the other routines of my days with her, as if after all nothing whatsoever had happened.

This is what's strangest about a separation like this: there's nothing to mark the occasion. You can't go to a funeral and afterwards, in a church basement, eat a macaroni hot dish you wouldn't normally touch. When your dog dies, you can grab a shovel and dig a hole, something else you don't normally do. But the morning I left Maryann, everything else went on amazingly as it had before, though at the outset, I intended otherwise.

With my jacket sleeve I brushed two inches of wet snow from the windshield of my car and then spun away from the curb just as on the days when I planned on returning. On those days, I didn't look back over my shoulder either.

I slid through a stop sign at the corner of our block where the paperboy was folding from a soggy bale our morning edition along with those of our neighbors on the street of brick-front walkups. Maryann and I had lived together there for one month shy of two years. I had a job. She had a cat we kept hidden from the landlord. I'd just paid the rent and the paperboy, so she'd have the *Trib* for two more weeks, our apartment for another month.

I wanted to go somewhere and eat macaroni hot dish.

Out on the highway, I drove south to the edge of the city where snow had turned to rain and trucks churned slush onto the hood of my car. I was going to Ohio with my clothes dangling from an aluminum bar across the back seat. Then momentarily, like the snow, my resolution lost its form. I drove to work instead, turning around at the last city exit and heading out of rain back into snow to the Conklin Furniture Factory, a three-story, block square building whose Florentine colonnaded façade gave it the appearance—from the front at least—of a public library, post office, or palace of a dislocated Tuscan lord.

I arrived an hour early, and mine being the first of two shifts, the plant was deserted, save for a watchman who peered at me from the distant window of the gluing department.

I left my car in its usual place and waded through slush to the rear of the plant and the railroad siding and wood scrap dump where we workers always smoked during our breaks. I had a notion of my life beginning over this day— something similar I felt the day the last of my parents died and the days I had been married and divorced. I thought I would have time on my hands now with Maryann off them.

I smoked a cigarette and picked among Conklin's wood scrap for some nicely grained oak pieces that had caught my eye the day before. By the time I returned to my car with a half dozen of these, my feet were wet, my pants wet to the knee, and my hands were numb. Other cars were in the parking lot then, and instead of being halfway to Ohio, I went to work for the last time coaxing Italian Provincial legs from a lathe, and—as luck would have it that morning—having my picture taken by a photographer who toured the plant with Tommy Conklin, the boss's son.

I cannot say precisely what was the attraction of wooden legs for one who had just given up Maryann's. It may have been, as perhaps was my impulsive detour to work that morning, no more than a habit asserting itself. Or maybe in my momentary absorption with fine southern oak, I reconsidered abstractly the flight I was taking from Maryann's ankles, calves, and thighs, for so long the furniture of my dreams.

Now and then I glanced at the clock on a wall at my back and imagined what Maryann might be doing at that moment: Maryann rolling over in the hide-a-bed, Maryann pulling the bag of cat food out from under the sink, Maryann gazing out upon the snow-splattered boulevard, then going back to bed.

I quit at noon and drove from Michigan to central Ohio in rain all the way. The incongruity of hanging around any longer caught up with me about the time that Maryann, a determined sleeper, would have been waking woozily for the second time and looking for the coffee I always left for her warm in a thermal carafe. My routines were so far intact that she would find it there today as well, but I worried that her subsequent discovery of my missing clothes and shaving gear would bring her down to the furniture plant to talk things over. Perhaps her heart didn't murmur after all. Perhaps it was premature of me to crave the macaroni hot dish that would end it all.

Once before she had followed me to work after a fight we'd had, strolling in with a hundred fifth-graders who happened to be there on a spring tour. They all wore yellow hard hats and plastic goggles, so I didn't recognize her until the others had filed past my lathe and she started saying things, shouting into my ear above the din of ten lathes and twice that many sanders nearby. "I'm sorry," she said.

"What?" I shouted.

"I'm sorry you slept on the floor last night," she said. She removed her goggles which had fogged over from her crying. She put her arms around my neck and wouldn't let go.

I tried to say soothing things, not so much because I felt that way but just to calm her. Whisper anything and it sounds sincere, but what is there like shouting our sentiments to make them sound plain silly? People ought to have to shout whatever they think of as heartfelt—lovers' vows, promises to change their ways, sincere regrets—all of it lofted in the air above some din. The world would be a different place.

Her hat fell off as I struggled to get her outside and into my car where I repeated everything I said in the plant to calm her. I spoke slowly this time, whispering, and this time it sounded beautiful. Maryann listened and was calmed. I kissed her nose and said I'd take the bus after work if she drove the car home.

Back in the plant, the men on the other lathes and sanders were laughing at me. They were still laughing during our coffee break as we smoked by the railroad tracks. I was a good sport, and this didn't bother me.

I told them the whole story. A train went by. Somebody said Maryann had nice knockers, and I agreed. We went back to work, but now a year later our breakup was past mending. I didn't want to have another scene with Maryann, so I told the foreman I was through and turned in my timecard at Conklin's office.

"You're camera shy, I suppose," said the payroll clerk in a voice as thick as her smears of eye shadow. Her last name was Morgan, and everybody called her Morgan only.

"No," I said, "I'm just shy in general." I winked at her. So much had my thoughts been on Maryann that I hardly considered Tommy Conklin and the photographer taking candid shots of us working at our lathes. I wasn't curious at all till Morgan reminded me.

"So what were the pictures all about?" I asked Morgan.

"Search me," said Morgan.

"I'd like to, Morgan," I said. Morgan was an old turkey with hair dyed the color of a carrot. We all said things like this to her, which she seemed to enjoy ignoring. She ignored me. Over her shoulder as she filled out some forms on the counter in front of me, I could see from her office window between Florentine columns, gathering heavy gray cloud and another snow squall moving in.

"It would have been nice if you'd given notice," she said. "I could have had all this done and waiting for you."

"Something came up," I said.

"It always does," said Morgan. "Sign here and here and here, Jack. She pushed the forms at me and rolled a pen across the counter. My name was written all over them, and I saw that I wasn't as far off the record as I thought. I signed three times without knowing what I was signing. I rolled the pen back to her.

"I'm moving out," I said.

She rolled the pen back to me. "Keep it," she said, "to remember us by." This time, *she* winked. The pen was inscribed with the Conklin name beneath a logo resembling the factory's colonnaded front. *"Specializing in fine Italian-style furniture."*

"Thanks, Morgan," I said. "I'll never forget you."

"Goodbye," she said. "Your health insurance will run out at the end of the month."

Looking out again over the top of her carrot hair, I saw that it was snowing hard now.

Ten minutes later I was back out on the highway, the snow was turning to rain south of the city again, and I was finally on my way to Ohio. Behind me, my clothes on metal hangers snuggled up together along the aluminum bar as my path veered right or left.

I settled with myself, since I didn't have a particular destination in mind, that I would stop the first place the rain stopped. The rain never stopped, nor did I see anything promising enough to make me stop regardless. At nightfall, the clouds were more uniformly thickened, and the rain increased.

I drove straight through Ohio, and still it was raining. I drank coffee at truck stops where diesel trailers glistened like reptiles on steaming sandbars. I picked up hitchhikers who talked for a mile and fell asleep. Their clothes dried in my car, and when they got as far as they were going, I let them out into the rain again. I drove with the big trucks snorting alongside me on the Interstate, rainwater hissing beneath my tires, with the smells of wet leather, wet blue jeans, and wet hair. Still it was raining.

Morning came with me across Indiana and into southern Illinois where plowed fields were underwater and canals formed between tree rows in peach orchards. I crossed the Mississippi River on a bridge that seemed to be gray iron on its east end and pewter on its west with the sun shining on it. Here, twenty miles from St. Louis, the rain had stopped, so twenty miles later I stopped. I had driven almost a thousand miles. Gutters were still awash and wet newspapers lay in flattened sheets upon sidewalks.

In St. Louis I found a room over a corner tavern in a section of the city where you could get drunk just walking around the block because every corner has its tavern, most of them run by families who live upstairs or in back rooms behind a drape door. From a family living behind such a door, I rented the only room upstairs where, otherwise, junk was stored. I had debris for neighbors: a retired juke box on the end of the hallway by the stairs, a room of empty beer cases from a defunct local brewery, two rooms of discarded bar furniture—upended Formica-top tables and steel chairs with red padded seats and backs.

I looked for a job, and, some nights, I walked around the block to check out the other corner taverns.

I bought a set of knives at a hobby store and began whittling bric-a-brac from the oak scraps I scavenged from Conklin's dump the day I quit. Sitting cross-legged on my bed and working by the light of a sign hanging outside over the tavern entrance, I carved miniature forms of familiar things.

I carved a fiddle my father had played in his amateur bluegrass band and then a lusty kingbird on a cottonwood bough outside our apartment in Michigan. I carved the cat Maryann and I had hidden so successfully from our landlord.

Out the window at evening's end I shook the shavings and wood chips from my blankets, but this never worked so well that I didn't find a few in bed with me among my scattered thoughts as I drifted off to sleep. From my open window came the buzz of bar talk down below, the smell of bratwurst frying. A polka might be played. On the old jukebox in the hallway was a stack of records from twenty years ago, all of them more recent than the polka, but still it was a polka.

I was in St. Louis a month when a letter came from Conklin's with my last payroll check and a note from Morgan. "Your girl came around asking for your address," Morgan wrote. "I didn't give it to her —privacy, you know."

To hell with privacy, I thought, and the next day sent Maryann my address, nothing more, written on a postcard of the St. Louis Arch. I had read somewhere that the biggest challenge in its construction was to make the two sides of it— built in stages curving toward each other—come out close enough to actually meet at the top. This struck me as a good metaphor for relationships like mine with Maryann.

I waited for a letter from her, peering out over the top of the tavern sign mornings and watching for the postman coming up the street. In my head

I composed replies to the various sorts of responses Maryann never sent: *Yes, I would come home. No, never. Yes, I'd send her money for half the electric bill as soon as I found a job. She shouldn't pay the paperboy for the two weeks I'd paid in advance. Maybe it was love after all. Maybe just a failure of engineering.*

I finished carving my wooden bric-a-brac, and as the days passed, I felt less and less like the lathe worker from a Michigan furniture plant. Now I carved memories instead of legs. Some things were never forgotten, and so, to that extent, records were kept, even by one who had avoided official ledgers. I quit watching for the postman. Atop the battered highboy in my room were my father's fiddle; the kingbird, looking not so lusty after all; and Maryann's cat, a little wobbly rearward as if just fallen from the womb.

I took a red chair from a vacant room down the hall and sat in it sometimes with my feet on the bed, facing the open window for a cool draft that never seemed to come as the days of late spring advanced into summer. Instead, there was always the smell of bratwurst frying till it sickened me, and the rattling of cicadas in neighborhood trees.

I couldn't find a job, and through the hot, wet

air of summer I seemed instead to search a sea bottom among the scuttled wrecks of ships with factory names. Finally I gave up and moved out two days before my next rent came due. I hung my clothes again on the aluminum bar across my car's back seat. I drove north to Minnesota. It was cooler there.

The day after Christmas a letter from Conklin's went to St. Louis and then followed me north. Inside were my payroll tax forms and another note from Morgan. "Something else to remember us by," she had scrawled across the margin of a page torn from a book. I thought of the pen she had given me the day I quit—lost now back in St. Louis.

The page was from a book called *Derby's Illustrated Reference*. Inset in a paragraph defining *lathe* was a small picture of me captioned *workman at lathe*. I'm wearing the gray shirt I pulled unironed from the bathroom doorknob the morning I left Maryann.

Though it's a small picture, I see that my collar lies more open at the neck than I like to have them. No starch there. My hands on the lathe are those of a workman all right. Confident and sure they seem, and my eyes seem intent on the leg I'm forming there. But I know better, of course. It was Maryann I was thinking about that morning.

Here is a picture of a man turning his life into memories, chewing his church-basement hot dish.

I forgot my little carvings on the highboy in St. Louis, but somewhere there's always a record left behind, I guess.

EARTHQUAKE

*C*arver was sipping brandy on ice when the earth began trembling in San Francisco. Ten minutes later, before the first news bulletins swept east, Eddie Hicks locked up his insurance agency and joined him in Miller's Bar while they waited for the five o'clock traffic to clear.

This was their habit every afternoon except Mondays when Carver's bank stayed open late, and he worked two extra hours supervising the installment loan department. Carver liked Mondays.

He wasn't much of a drinker, so the four days a week he and Eddie waited out the traffic in a bar, he didn't have a drink at home. But Monday evening, he sipped brandy on ice in the living room with his wife Bernice, two before dinner and a glass of sherry afterwards. He enjoyed this. He had remained comfortable with his wife through a marriage of thirty-one years.

He sometimes wished he could turn his routine around to drink four afternoons a week with Bernice instead.

Now that their two children were grown and living out of state, it was possible to be alone with Bernice once again—no television or stereo blaring, no sweat socks on the stairs, no phone calls from his daughter's friends to disturb the depth of silence he soaked in like a soothing bath. After twenty years, he could once more hear the hallway clock ticking all hours, and though he cared about his children and fondly recalled their boisterous antics, he cherished that clock with the unabashed regard that shy people reserve for pets and inanimate things. This heirloom from his mother's side had labored with him through decades of hubbub to sound again with the steady, unbroken resonance of an old truth he lost track of for a while and then rediscovered.

But this being Wednesday afternoon, Carver seemed no closer to that than to the trembling earth in San Francisco. Miller's Bar had swelled like a bean in the rain, the sort of cold, filmy drizzle that drives people to drink with its insinuations of worse to come—a snowstorm by supper, pneumonia this weekend. Carver surveyed the bedlam around him: faces yellow in yellow bar light; ties seeming to strangle in their constricting turns the very necks they adorned; yellow arms raised in the gestures of drowning folk; a television elevated in a distant corner flashing pictures without sound. He couldn't help wondering what he was doing here when it all seemed more hopeless than the weather, more congested than the traffic he'd wanted to avoid.

Carver gave his friend an incriminating glance as if it weren't his own fault he was here again. He wished that habits weren't so hard to break. Bernice had complained of stomach pains this morning and again at noon when he called her, and he ought to have gone straight home after work. Instead, here he was with Eddie, an old habit. In a minute or so, he would get up and call Bernice again from a pay phone by the men's room, just to check in and see how she felt.

Eddie was having trouble getting his first drink. The waitress went by him twice, even faster the second time when he shouted to get her attention.

"And the business we give this place ... the tips we drop—" he muttered. He slouched in his chair and began munching crackers from a plastic bowl in the center of their table. He seemed not so much to chew them as to swallow them half at a time, bitten on the diagonal.

Carver looked at Eddie and included him in the category of hopeless things he saw here, a thirsty man devouring salty crackers. Then he looked away at the silent television where a cartoon gorilla shambled after a cartoon duck. The gorilla was orange. He waved in his hand a club the color and shape of an overdone turkey drumstick. He was faster than the duck, but he chased an acrobat. With a lightning dodge between the ape's legs, the duck escaped being brained just as Eddie's drink came.

During time out for a candy commercial, Carver saw that the cartoon show was called *The Children's Hour*—a Longfellow poem he had memorized in grade school. He could still recall bits of it, though the flesh and blood details of the part of his life to which it belonged had rotted off and fallen away. Had he been given a birthday party the year he memorized it? He couldn't recall his gifts, if so, or what games they played, or most of his friends who might have come. Had the summer been cold and rainy as some were, or hot and broken by afternoon showers like others he knew lay behind him? Had it been a year of rainbows or of whirlwinds stirring dust in the alley behind his house? When had his Brittany spaniel been run over?

"Carver, you look positively gloomy. What's on your mind, old boy? The bank didn't fail today, did it?"

"I was thinking about my Brittany spaniel."

"I thought you had a setter."

"A long time ago when I was a kid—"

"—and another for my friend here," Eddie shouted. He pointed to Carver's empty glass and dropped a fifty on the waitress's tray. Having sold an expensive policy just this afternoon, he felt like a tycoon. "A hundred thou of whole life," he said to Carver as the waitress spun away to another table.

Carver nodded, forced a smile, and found in Eddie's news yet more reason for melancholy. This went deeper than the dumb spectacle of a gorilla chasing a duck in a bar on a rainy afternoon with nobody watching—that days like this, insurance should sell as well as booze. There was something mortally frail in the smell of soggy trash in window wells, in wool coats drying too close to heat registers.

Who wouldn't distill out of such a day as this the need to place a wager with the ticking clock? On days like this, even the gently swaying pendulum in the machine in his upstairs hallway demanded a hedge against time pulling the rug out.

Carver tried to imagine *whole life,* a hundred thousand worth divided into the years and weeks he'd lived with Bernice, the minutes and split seconds of all that time, the small change of private moments. Dimes and quarters clinked in the air around him. Drinks were bought and sold. Life insurance was melancholy indeed. So was its salesman buying his friend brandy on the long-range odds most of us bet foolishly when we bought whole life.

On television, the chase resumed with variations while Carver watched, hummed replies to Eddie's chatter, and mused his way through life insurance back to Longfellow's poem. The gorilla with a landing net, the gorilla with a bulldozer, the duck igniting explosives in his path. "Between the dark and the daylight," the first line of *The Children's Hour.*

"Maybe you're just tired, old boy," Eddie said. He was a fat man with the enflamed face and heavy lips of an alcoholic nightclub comedian. The more insurance he sold, the redder and fatter he seemed to get. Liquor and a high starch diet had nothing to do with it. Whole life and tax shelters fed his flames, the pathetic distillation of sodden afternoons in the city.

"I should call my wife," Carver said. He got up and pushed his way through a crowd to the men's room pay phone. From Longfellow's poem he recalled something about the sun going down, the light going out of everything, a man trying to rest…. He let the phone ring ten times, counting them; Bernice didn't answer. He forgot his change in the return slot.

"I wonder where my wife is," he said to Eddie.

Eddie shrugged, thumbed through the change from his fifty. His friend was such a wet blanket today he no longer felt like a tycoon.

The gorilla's bulldozer careened wildly off the road and into a forest, flattening trees in equal number to right and left. Carver wasn't a reader these days. He hadn't thought of Longfellow for a long time, and he would have been surprised to hear that almost nobody read such a poet any-more, almost nobody took Longfellow seriously. He thought he would look for his poem in the public library one of these days. He'd never get it all from memory when a stint in the army, a wife, two children grown up, and thirty years of banking intervened. He shared a fate with the gorilla who would never get his duck.

They both chased things perpetually elusive— a duck, a poem, for a long time the sound of an ancient mechanism rolling its gears outside his bedroom door. Always there were interruptions, digressions, times when things turned around, and the damn duck chased you, a chase even now suspended by the network flashing first word of the San Francisco earthquake. Somebody nudged the bartender who turned off the music, turned up the sound.

"I'll never understand the Richter Scale," said Eddie. "Does that sound like a bad one to you?"

"Bad," said Carver. "A calamity."

"Jesus, what do you know? Those claims office people out there will be catching hell tomorrow."

Carver wondered what had happened to shake him so, to the very heart of him. How could an earthquake so far away do that? She might have been a hundred places away from the phone. Music returned, the gorilla returned with the duck on the bulldozer after him now. Of course, tables turned and turned again.

Some elemental tension in the earth had lain

out of sight for ages, conserving itself while machines ripped and tore at the soil on rocks far above, while men came to mortice bricks and blocks, to asphalt over the scars of their work. Steel girders and hanging glass probed the sky at last. But the fault remained, the rocks would slip, the tension release inevitably, and Carver felt as though this tremor reached through mountains and across deserts to rattle in his heart. Somewhere in his moral landscape, a crevice opened up. From its edge he peered, awestruck, down into its depths.

"Hey, where are you going?" Eddie asked, laying a heavy hand on his as he got up from their table.

"Home," Carver said, pulling free. "I want to see if Bernice is alright."

"For God's sake, Carver. That quake is a thousand miles from here!" Eddie shouted after him.

In front of his house when he got there, an ambulance was just pulling away from the curb, its red lights spinning out chromatic reflections in front windows on both sides of the block, in rain slicks on the street. Ross Barnet, a next-door neighbor, stood under the gas lamp on Carver's front lawn, his face and hands as yellow as any he had just left behind in Miller's Bar. He pointed toward the ambulance and shouted something Carver understood without hearing it through the rain, the slap of his windshield wipers, the wail of the siren.

He chased the ambulance back downtown, past his bank, and then up into the hills on the other side where a new hospital had been built.

Bernice lingered there a night, then a day with their daughter Sylvia flying in from Toledo, another night with their son Tom driving from Freebourg, and Sylvia saying to her father outside the surgery wing where they sat on a bench in an alcove, "You're probably wondering why I came here alone."

Carver shook his head, but that didn't stop her.

"We're getting a divorce." She whispered this as if she feared her mother would overhear from beyond the double doors to their left under a cloud of anesthetic three operating rooms away.

Carver smiled without giving this news much thought. He wasn't happy to hear his daughter's marriage was breaking up. He smiled because he had just recalled a line from another poem he read long ago. It fit so well:

"*With their triumphs and their glories and the rest*," he said to Sylvia, "*love is best.*"

She studied him through large, dark eyes, her mother's eyes, except that they seemed to say he was crazy, and they managed to be cold in their pools of eye shadow where Bernice's had always been warm. Yet despite all the ice Carver saw there, they left off staring at him and wept just as Tom came running down the hall.

Bernice was slowly bleeding to death, and even now, through the second surgery in a day, no doctor in the city knew how to stop it. The next morning, before sunrise, she died.

Leaving his children behind to tend to details in the hospital, Carver stepped out into an empty street where the dawn was still not strong enough to cast shadows. He drove home and put his car in the garage. He let the dog out of the kennel. Two newspapers lying inside the screen door he kicked ahead of him into the kitchen.

He poured a glass of brandy without ice, and in the living room where he sipped it, the morning sun flamed through a front window whose drapes hadn't been drawn shut in three days. Out there in the glare, his next-door neighbor crossed a slice of lawn between his driveway and the sidewalk leading to his door. Help was on the way.

Carver could hear his old clock ticking in the

hallway upstairs behind him. Out in the kitchen in one of the newspapers drying and slowly unfolding itself on the floor, a headline read, "Nobody Killed in West Coast Quake."

Carver set his glass aside, covered his face with his hands. The front doorbell rang.

THE END OF THE END OF
THE WORLD

*E*ver since my wife ran away with my daughter's violin teacher, I have been sitting in bars, drinking beer and eating Polish sausage on a bun, which any good bar around here can fix. I have also been suffering from a condition I cannot identify by name, but it is the opposite of amnesia. Instead of forgetting, which I take to the be the normal course anyway—even if hastened by a blow on the head—I am remembering.

My past is assembling around me. I see old faces and the contours of distant landscapes in my history: my birthday party when I was six; hitchhiking to Yellowstone the summer after high school graduation; the knobby growth on my grandfather's left thumb; the ivy plant hanging in his kitchen.

The old faces I see in this bar just now belong to my friends from long ago. Of course, I am possibly mistaken. These faces may be instead the creations of my chagrin—the distorted fantasies of a man who lost out to a violin teacher—but I will tell you what I see regardless.

A bit more jowl I see, sideburns and mustache, a frosty wig over the gold ringlets I recall, but these are still people I knew from years ago, and were I less timid in my new condition of remembering, I would get down from my barstool and greet them.

"Hello," I would say to Marvin who hangs his head alone in a distant corner booth. "Remember ten years ago in Pittsburg? I insured my first car with you."

"Hello," to Brenda who married my college roommate. I was their best man. She wears glasses now and a frosty wig. She didn't drink solo in the old days, but here is Brenda all right, this Friday afternoon in Kermit's Bar with the November sun setting.

"Hello," to Leonard sitting next to me. *Doc* we used to call him. He played a good clarinet. He chewed his reeds when he got nervous. I thought he died in Wichita, but here—this afternoon—I could tug at Leonard's coat sleeve.

Even now, to test the matter, I hold my hand near him, palm down, fingers extended, in yellow bar light like harvest moonlight. Mine is the hand of a man who works in offices, who wears suits and ties, but still a man's hand, I believe, though outstretched near Leonard's arm, it trembles as though a ghost were seen.

I remember touching my grandfather's arm with trembling fingers as he lay in his casket. The knobby growth on his thumb was visible but softened in its lines and receding gently as his face was also then. I recoil from Leonard as I recoiled then, awed and transfixed by facts that don't make sense: the dead alive; the living dead; a clarinet player; a grandfather; a wife; a violin teacher.

My hands seek out the cool, moist sides of my beer glass. My fingers wrap around it, intermingle for comfort, and in my beer an amber fountain rises before me cradled in glass above the black laminated bar top. My grandfather arises from the black earth he husbanded and walks once more behind his plow. I stare at the rising, beaded effervescence and remember other things as well. Side by side, two bubbles rise into the milky beer head. Two memories of my college days surface.

One is Amelia Noble, a girl I secretly loved but spoke to only once, and the other is a prediction that the world would end Friday afternoon. Amelia was in a dozen of my college classes scattered over four years, and with alphabetical seating, sat beside me in most of them. The news of Armageddon I heard from an itinerant preacher named Dr. Boynton who came to town in late October of my freshman year. His clarion was a loudspeaker mounted atop an old blue bus, and through it—at every intersection in town—he announced with tinny screams the call to Judgement. That semester, I sat with Amelia Noble in Western Civilization. All I remember from that class was that Saint Anthony became a monk in Egypt, fasted, and lived alone to the age of one-hundred and five.

Amelia Noble was the prettiest girl I ever knew. She was also the most intelligent. Dr. Boynton brought to town with him a 10x20-foot canvas painting rolled and tied like a rug on the top of his bus. He summoned his followers to a nightly meeting in an open meadow west of the college. From his bus, he unpacked floodlights and an electric organ. He had a fat young woman to play it. He unfolded a speaker's platform of hinged planking. He untied the painted canvas and staked it up like a baseball backstop behind him on the open field. He cranked an old diesel engine which shuddered and hissed and sputtered life into the floodlights, the organ, and even it seemed into the fat young woman who beamed radiance and played a swollen chord.

But especially did life surge into the canvas stretched glowing at Dr. Boynton's back with his dancing shadow in preacher's postures projected double and triple upon it in the crossfire of spotlights.

Amelia Noble had blue eyes which I first noticed for a trace of moisture in them suggesting tenderness, but turning out to be hard glitter. Her eyes were metallic and black at their centers—upholstery tacks reducing me to stuffed furniture. She kept pinned in me words I might easily have spoken to a hundred other girls. In my throat was so much wadding under her gaze, and as we sat through Chemistry and Contemporary Social Problems, it matted and lost its spring. Side by side, we sat with the atomic chart evolving before us. A post-war culture became urban. The family farm was dead, and I was speechless.

Out on the college meadow, Dr. Boynton waved his arms. His body shook. His shadows gyrated across the canvas, and in moments when the light coursed out between them, one could see details of the Last Judgement: a great white cloud looming in the east; lots of flaming sunbeams and cirrus wisps painted along the fringe; caroling angels arrayed above; the saintly robed in white gathered upon the billowy plateau; the already damned skulking in a murky corner beneath; and foreground center, the throng summoned to final account.

In Philosophy with Amelia Noble, we learned the allegory of Plato's chariot—the driver and the wild steeds he held in check, reason and the passions under its control. My silence with Amelia was elevated to art and made a truth. In Music Appreciation, we listened to an old musicologist recall Rachmaninoff performing in concert.

"His hands were those of a farm boy," the old musicologist said. "Too clumsy, I thought, for the piano. Then he played…."

Four years passed this way. There were theories and concepts, methods of analysis and distribution, techniques and execution, style; and I have wondered in the ten years since, how a man could be silent for so long in the presence of his love.

"How?" I ask, whispering insistently to the bubbles in my beer. "Leonard, back from the grave, *Tell me what you know of silence.* Grandfather, behind the plow, *Were Rachmaninoff's hands okay?*"

My college dormitory emptied three nights running for Dr. Boynton's revival meetings. Most of us students stayed at the fringe of the crowd and well clear of the central frenzy of believers who thrust forward until Dr. Boynton's plank platform blocked their way. They stomped and moaned and seemed to summon out of the earth the very ground fog that rolled in upon them as the night air cooled. They became an extension of the painted throng on Dr. Boynton's canvas, the fog an extension of his Judgement cloud, Dr. Boynton himself upon his platform rising above it like the Redeemer.

Shafts of sunlight through the high French Gothic windows of old Montclair Hall and an ocean of dust motes floated over our heads as Amelia Noble and I, on folding chairs, sat together for the last time. We were but two of at least a thousand. In our ears for almost an hour throbbed the graduation roll. What is there like a long list of names to make rubbish of private worth?

My eyes sought out the vaulted ceiling, and I went to sea among the dust motes. I had by this time the habit of Amelia silently at my side, and I do not recall even thinking then that this would be the end for us. Once or twice, I tried to focus my thoughts on the names we heard, but I couldn't keep with it.

A familiar name floated to the surface of my attention; then came the blending and blurring, the unvariegated voice of the college dean in counterpoint with the tramping of feet in the graduation line. Manfred *Somebody* was awarded the Degree of Bachelor of Science. I heard this and a slurry of other names, but momentarily there was a new ingredient in this blend, a whisper in my ear. Amelia Noble had broken the silence of four years. I turned my eyes aslant to hers, conscious that I looked ridiculous with a graduation tassel then hanging between them.

"Manfred," Amelia said to me. I brushed the tassel aside. "I would not give any baby of mine that name."

"Same here," I whispered in reply.

"Same here," was all I ever said to Amelia Noble, and I cannot imagine anything more inane that I might have said instead. Across our laps and folded hands, the same sunlight lay, flooding through the Gothic windows of a high romance, and the girl I thought to be all upholstery tacks and analysis had just spoken to me of her babies.

My eyes sought out again the dust-mote sea where once more I went adrift, and nowhere in it could I find another word for Amelia Noble. We sat through the remaining ceremony like a couple at a divorce hearing. Someone read Frost's "Stopping by Woods." An organ tugged at us with the sonorous, swelling tones of a Recessional, and we arose, a thousand at once from our folding chairs.

Up in the balcony of Montclair Hall, was it Dr. Boynton's fat young woman I saw in a nest of pipes as we paraded down the main aisle? Then I saw the great double oak door standing open to the noon day. Passing through, I saw its inlaid, engraved brass plates. I both saw and felt the sunlight flooding full upon the steps as we descended. Then our ranks broke, and I never saw Amelia again.

On Tuesday evening, the second of his revival, Dr. Boynton had announced that the world would end by Friday afternoon, and as I heard this from a distant grove of trees, I stumbled over a couple making love. Dr. Boynton could create a frenzy, but he was no match in my attention for a bare rump pointing toward the stars. I ran away and missed the fog rolling in that night.

The next day, I went out to the meadow later and kept clear of the trees. Fewer students milled curiously at the crowd's fringe by then, but believers were more numerous than ever, and three times I heard Dr. Boynton's prediction.

"Friday, as the sun reaches its zenith, this will all end," he said in choking spasms. He waved his right arm over the crowd, over his blue bus, and over the fat girl who fingered a tremolo on the organ. He pointed to the painted canvas at his back. "Friday, you will be judged with all your friends," he said, "and visible to all eyes will be the shameful secrets of your unreported sins."

From the organ broke a thunderclap, but I kept thinking about the white rump I had seen last evening among the trees.

It seems to me that first place in our memories belongs inevitably to such compelling and incidental visions where we seem to witness as framed pictures the unrefined facts of our existence. These pictures are what we most likely recall—for no reason, day or night, a dozen years later even—and could we live so long, we might awaken before the dawn of another century with just these pictures in mind.

The white rump is one such for me, and the warty growth on my grandfather's thumb is another. I have gazed out my office window on certain afternoons and seen both floating over the downtown skyline. I have also seen, like twin moons floating in the same sky, the full, dumb eyes of a cow my grandfather's neighbor hit square in the skull with a sledgehammer to kill for butchering. I can see any time the colony of white slugs that had eaten the heart out of an aspen tree and felled it across a picnic table not three feet from where I sat. I remember the twisted root of my first wisdom tooth, a remnant of my jaw flesh still clinging to it. I remember the cockroach in my bowl of cornflakes and my wife in the arms of the violin teacher the afternoon I came home early from work. I remember the eyes and face of Amelia Noble.

Both Wednesday and Thursday evenings, Dr. Boynton repeated his prediction, but by this time, most of the college students had tired of him and stayed away. Thursday evening, the crowd of believers seemed smaller as well. Perhaps, after all, Dr. Boynton had misunderstood the forces that drive people to and fro.

The news of Armageddon did not awaken hearts: it deadened them. We might maintain our delight in the same song over and over, in the same chord on Dr. Boynton's organ, and we could contemplate the same flower blooming through a lifetime of springs. We are most easily bored by repetition of the colossal, a herd of elephants joined trunk and tail in the circus ring while drums pound. In another ring, a clown sleeping in a child's coaster wagon steals the show.

I had to see it Friday, with the sun approaching its zenith, but I was alone out on the college meadow to witness the world's end. Not even Dr. Boynton was there, having skulked out of town in advance of his own prophecy, and in that narrow sense alone, he had made his own words come true. The blue bus, the folding stage, the organ and the fat girl, the painted Judgement canvas, the crowd itself—these things had all departed, as he said they would. Perhaps the world didn't end all at once, but just piece by piece, a little more of it going away every day. One day, a beaming fat girl went, another Rachmaninoff and my grandfather. After that went Amelia Noble and then my wife. Every day we became emptier in ways.

Across the vacant meadow, I had walked at noontime. The brown autumn grass was trampled into the red clay. I could see across my path the tracks of Dr. Boynton's blue bus meandering out to the street. Where the Judgement painting had been, a broken stake pointed. Judgement lay that way, and out on the street, traffic hurtled in Dr. Boynton's trail—trucks and buses of other hues and shades, multitudes of cars. A few more years, and I was out there with them.

I moved north after graduation, found a job, and married a secretary from the office. She ran away last week. I sit around bars and eat polish sausage. I count the bubbles in my glass of beer. I talk to dead men. I remember.

THE HARDWARE MAN

"*I* won't touch them. They're icky," Tyler said, recoiling from the display case of used electric razors.

"Icky, for God's sake, what kind of a word is that?" McTandy shouted in his nephew's ear.

"As good as any. I used it in a poem once."

If McTandy ever thought of poetry, it was as Mother Goose. He sneered. "I've heard little girls use it around caterpillars, and even they had more gumption than you. Dust those razors or get out of my store."

"I'll get out then," Tyler said with a simpering voice. He had a knowing look McTandy found threatening. "I'll get out," he repeated. He raised his eyes to the ceiling, and McTandy knew what he meant. Upstairs was McTandy's apartment and his wife. What would *she* think? Tyler, the precocious devil, already knew enough to ask him that and call his bluff.

McTandy retreated to a distant wall where he was hanging wrenches on pegboard hooks. He had the feeling he was whipped. "Afraid of electric razors," he muttered to himself. "The kid must be goofy on drugs."

Tyler was his wife's nephew, and her insistence had won him a summer job helping out in the hardware store. She would flay him if he fired Tyler the first day. Besides, he had come in on a jet from Ohio with a one-way ticket. McTandy would have to keep him long enough to earn his way back at least. The problem was to get rid of him even then.

He was sixteen. McTandy discovered that much about him when he pled child labor laws with his wife.

"He's sixteen," she said, "so he's old enough, and the laws don't apply to close relatives anyway." She tapped a spoon on their kitchen table and spoke like a judge.

McTandy had not so much as met the boy, and his wife was scarcely better informed. She based her faith in Tyler's good character on a moment's visitation at his cribside the year before she married McTandy and moved to St. Louis where they started his hardware business. "He was a cute baby," she said.

McTandy knew better than dispute her logic. They had no children of their own, and he thought she blamed him for it. "He'll have long hair, I'll bet, a regular hippie."

"McTandy," she said, "you go to J.C. Penney and see those boys working. They have hair on their shoulders. It's good enough for Penney's, and those boys aren't even family."

"You can't trust hippies."

"It's family, McTandy."

He was beaten and knew it. He went downstairs to his store, and his wife wrote Tyler a letter. That was a week ago, and now Tyler was working his first day in the store. Blond hair was hanging down his back in disordered curls when it wasn't hanging in his face. He was saying words like icky and, for all McTandy knew, hallucinating over used electric razors. He hung another wrench on a hook and peered cautiously over his shoulder. Tyler had fled the razors. He was in front of the store by the cash register. McTandy dropped a handful of wrenches among the bins of chisels and screwdrivers as he pursued his nephew.

"What are you doing here?" he gasped between breaths. He had expected to find an empty till and Tyler on his way out the door to buy drugs. Instead, he bent over the counter writing with a short pencil on a strip of cash register tape. He raised a hand, implying that he didn't want to be bothered, and kept on writing.

"Listen here," McTandy said. "I don't know what you're up to, but it ain't work. Now are you going to work or not?"

Tyler wrote another line and looked up through matted strands of hair. "I just wrote a poem," he said.

"Like hell you did," McTandy said. "Not on my time, for my pay."

"There it is," he said, pointing to some words scribbled on the cash register tape. "Do you want to read it?"

"Where's the broom?"

Tyler shrugged and began to read. He had a nasal voice, and when he spoke, his upper lip protruded slightly, an affectation that made him resemble a flute player. "It's called 'Electric Memory'."

"Where's the broom?" McTandy asked again,

but this time his voice was low and secretive. The bell over his front door had just rung and a customer was coming in.

Tyler pushed the hair from his eyes and looked up again. "I don't know," he said. "I just got started."

McTandy laughed for the benefit of his customer, but his eyes were feral. "That's the trouble, Tyler," he whispered. "You haven't started. Otherwise, you'd know about the broom. Understand?" He pointed toward the back of the store. "It's by the alley door. Give the aisles a good sweeping, and when you're finished, dust those razors." He laughed again and then looked around for his customer, an old lady who carried a straw handbag under her arm. "Mrs. Hurst," he sang out. "How are you today?"

In their apartment upstairs, his wife sat down at her piano. She played it every morning, always at the same time, always the same songs she learned long ago in school, always beginning with "A Song of India" which seemed to be her favorite. They were melancholy, mournful songs for the most part, evocative of romantic love and life's sorrows. McTandy hated them, and because her playing sifted down into his store, he heard them over and over, a distant hollow sound like an old record reverberating in an empty room. He thought them wretched, lonely songs to fill a hardware store with. They muted the happy bell above his door, and each morning descended like a dirge over him and his business. Dust falling on his shelves, a cat whining at his alley door, these he could control. Where his wife was concerned, he was helpless.

Years ago, he had dared to complain, but he was at heart a weak, uncertain man whose loud words could be ignored. His wife knew this and ignored him. "McTandy," she once said, "you bark a lot." He was enraged but went down to the hardware in silence. Whenever he was angry with her, at any time of day or night, he descended to the hardware. He never fought it out with her or anyone else. His hardware had always been his domain, the apartment hers, and he never forgot that she lived above him. When it wasn't her piano he heard, it was just her movements, her footsteps on the floor over his head. And when he heard nothing at all, he thought she eaves-dropped.

Behind him Tyler was pushing a broom up and down the aisles. He might have been a minor key metamorphosed from his wife's piano. Mc-Tandy could do nothing about him, perhaps, but at least Tyler's song would end. He had but to wait out the summer and do what he could to avoid trouble.

A customer sometimes noticed the piano. "Oh, do you hear it?" McTandy would say, cocking his head to one side and listening. "You have good ears. I can't hear it at all." If they noticed Tyler, he would say, "I hardly know he's here, but it's only for the summer."

Hardware was McTandy's business, and he drifted in it like a man who married poorly and went to sea for peace of mind. He clung to his tools and his bolts and his cast iron skillets. They were his iron-clad ship, unalterable and solid in any weather. He would sometimes take a heavy wrench in his hand just to heft it. "There, feel that," he would say to himself. "Now, isn't that something, how solid it is?" Here was matter that would not change in his grasp, like a woman in marriage, like a cute baby come to torment him with his long hair and insolence.

McTandy's was a neighborhood business of south St. Louis. He sold to people he knew for a dozen blocks around, people who were as badly worn down as the houses they lived in. They were mostly old and mostly poor and unlikely to be lured among suburban discount stores. They came to him instead when they needed a pound of nails, a rubber washer, a hank of rope. He made a quiet, steady living by it, and that was just what he expected from hardware.

He liked to call his customers by their first names, and because he thought it good for business, he did more than any close friend would. If they wished to call him Ralph, so much the better. But it was usually McTandy they called him, since he was one of those men who went comfortably by his last name. Even he thought so. And as old customers died or moved away, others moved in to replace them—usually to replace the dead ones, because in this part of the city it was easier to die than move out. Either way, McTandy learned the names of the new and forgot the old and kept his nose close to his hardware.

As the weeks went by to the end of this summer, he discovered that Tyler had two interests. He would push a broom and write verse on cash register tape. An hour every morning and afternoon, he pushed the broom up and down his aisles. He leaned heavily into the handle and trudged along as though the world were in his way. Back and forth he labored until McTandy's floor was polished stone. In between, he sat on a high stool near the alley door, where McTandy moved him, alternately chewing on his pencil and writing verse on tape, carefully rolling it back on the spool at the end of the day. By midsummer, he was spending half his time unwinding and winding the tape to get at the part he was writing. While he worked, it lay all about in coils and ringlets, gray with pencil marks and a foot deep around the stool.

Sometimes McTandy would pause in his work to study him. Sometimes Tyler would brush the hair from his face and look up. If their eyes met, McTandy was always the first to look away. Tyler had a long, mournful face and large, sad cow's eyes. McTandy learned to appreciate the hair that so often kept them from view.

Every day he ordered Tyler to dust the secondhand razors, a display of twenty or so in an open-backed glass counter. He had them arranged in three rows there, each upright in its case with a white card in front to reveal its age and price. Every day Tyler refused to go near them, and dust drifting in from behind the counter lay like ash on every one of them because McTandy had more pride than to do it himself as long as Tyler remained in his store.

Electric razors were the only used merchandise McTandy bothered with. He bought them cheap, reconditioned them himself if they needed it, and sold them at a good profit. He bought maybe ten a year, and he sold about that many, so he always had twenty or so on hand. He acquired them from women, chiefly widows disposing of their husbands' effects, men of the neighborhood whose names he had known, who themselves had come to his store often enough before their razors came there without them. For a while after he bought one, he thought of it by the name of the man who owned it. He avoided such references in his talk with customers, but he could not dust the razors himself or even pass by the counter without thinking that this was Eddie's or that Bob's and the old Schick was Foster's. Such things passed in time, however, taking more or less long in relation to how well he had known the men, and as the months went by, he began to confuse the names, and finally he forgot them.

Summers were usually slow times for the razor business. He did a good trade in vacuum bottles, flashlight batteries, and fly tapes, but it was poor for razors. Most of these he bought in the fall and sold just before Christmas. It seemed to him that men of the neighborhood were likely to die at any time, a few more in March after a hard winter perhaps, but there was no real pattern to it as far as he could see. Yet no matter what the month or season, their widows were most likely to come in autumn if they ever came at all with an electric razor to sell. They started showing up after the first frost, when leaves were yellow and grass brown, and the wind was blowing loose dirt and dry paper in swirls around lampposts. They started then and stopped before Thanksgiving. He would have made a bet on it.

And so Mrs. Hurst was an exception when she returned to his store in August. She hadn't been there since Tyler's first day, and now it was nearly his last. McTandy recalled that with some satisfaction when the bell above his door rang, and she tottered in. He remembered her distinctly as the first customer to see Tyler. He remembered his happiness when she ignored him, even though she left without buying anything. Now he wondered who would be the last to see his nephew.

Mrs. Hurst had the straw bag under her arm this time as well, and McTandy greeted her in the usual fashion. She was a small old lady with slate-gray, beetle eyes, a wire-thin nose, and yellow hair tucked unevenly under a kerchief she wore drawn up tight at the point of her chin.

"McTandy," she said, ignoring his greeting, "I want a word with you."

He stepped back in surprise and looked for his nephew near the alley door. Tyler was safely out of the way on his stool and half concealed within spiraling folds of cash register tape.

"What's the trouble, Mrs. Hurst?" he asked in his best voice which was just then none too good.

"This." She fumbled in her straw bag and drew out an electric razor. She held it to his face.

"This?" he asked, looking cross-eyed at it just beyond the tip of his nose. "What's wrong with it?"

"I bought it for Henry last Christmas."

"Yes," he said, "I remember." He didn't remember, but it seemed a small concession to please her. "Is it broken?"

"No, but Henry's neck is. He's dead since yesterday, and I want to sell it back to you."

McTandy's long experience with widows failed him. He stammered something unintelligible about his sorrow.

She cut him short. "You needn't, McTandy. I've already had enough of being sorry from others. I felt that way myself until I woke up alone this morning. I'm an old lady, and I don't have much time left for anything, even being sorry. A day to me is as much as a year to that youngster back there." She pointed to Tyler with the razor. He sat on his stool with lowered head. Then she brought the razor to her own face and looked at it as though she were speaking to Henry. "Behind my back they'll all say I drove him to it anyway. But it was a dirty thing for him to do, to die like that and leave me alone with not a penny to pay the undertaker. So, I'm going to sell his stuff to bury him. I paid ten dollars for this razor, and that's what I want back. It ain't been used a year, and Henry never shaved every day either."

McTandy would have given a hundred to have her out of his store. He rushed to his cash register, groped for a ten-dollar bill, and handed it to her. She put the razor on his counter and next to it a brown leather case she also took from her straw bag. "It come with it," she said.

She made her slow way to the door. The bell was tinkling above her head as she turned to McTandy once more. "Did Henry buy some rope here Monday?"

McTandy nodded, recalling it now, but already wishing he couldn't.

"Well, that's what he hung himself with." She went out the door with the ten dollars clenched in her white, boney fist.

McTandy thought the bell would never stop ringing. For what seemed a long time afterward, he stood by his cash register and stared at it. It rang as long as he stared, and he stared until Tyler spoke. He had walked up the aisle with a strip of tape trailing behind him to the alley door and swishing against the counter sides as he moved.

"I told you they were icky," he said. "They're dead men's. I wouldn't touch them. You put them against your face and feel cold, just like—" He turned away and walked back to his stool, picking up the tape as he went. "—just like dead men," he said over his shoulder. He moved slowly down the aisle, pausing with every step to catch up the loose tape in his hands. McTandy watched him in dumb silence. Overhead, he could hear his wife's piano, and it seemed to vibrate in his heart with the bell. Tyler climbed up on his stool and shouted, "You should have read the poem."

That was the last thing McTandy could recall Tyler saying to him. He must have said other things before he went away, but for the rest of the week, McTandy in his hardware was a man wandering in a desert. He roamed aimlessly up and down the aisles, sometimes stopping and looking about the walls and counters as though he had lost something and hoped to find it there. He paid little attention to Tyler, his wife, or his customers. He took money, wrapped packages, and made change the same way he got out of bed, ate his meals, and went back to bed. It was all habit and all the same to him. His wife thought he was sick and told him so every time he sat down to a meal. He nodded his head and mumbled a denial.

Tyler left early Saturday morning with his suitcase in one hand and the roll of cash register tape in the other. McTandy's wife held the front door for him and went along to the airport. The bell rang above them and the door closed. Tyler looked back through its glass and waved, holding the tape in his hand like a large lifesaver. He pressed his nose against a front window and waved again before he went away. McTandy was alone in his store.

For the first time all summer he was alone there, and he didn't like it any longer. His eyes meandered among the shadowy counters. With the lights still off, his wrenches gleamed in an amber city dawn washing through his front windows. Between the wrenches was darkness, and between his counters the aisles were murky. He stood by the display of razors, and his eyes kept wandering back to them through the darkness and the distant glitter. They were obscure in the dim light, in the gray dust drifted over them. He could just discern their silhouettes in rows, and it seemed to him that he stood before a cemetery, each razor a stone, on each stone a name and dates he could read if only he turned on the lights and disturbed the dust of dead men.

There is in this part of the city a scavenger, an old man who trudges up and down the alleys pushing a two-wheeled buggy like a fruit vendor's cart before him. Usually he comes alone, but sometimes he brings a woman. She helps him rummage through the trash. She may be his wife. This morning when he comes abreast McTandy's alley door he will find among the garbage can a box of electric razors and a high wooden stool. Fearing some mistake, he will fling them into his cart and not return for many weeks.

BIG-HEARTED BOZO

*B*ozo was not his real name. That was *Bosso*, from a central European name, corrupted and lopped-off, and then in Bozo's case mispronounced for so many years as a nickname that even Eugene Bosso thought of himself as Bozo.

He was a short, skinny man with thick black hair he wore all brushed to one side, standing up and then folding over on itself like the comb of an old hen. His dark eyes glistened and could not have looked tentatively at so much as a snowflake.

Bozo sold cold cuts over the road. He drove refrigerated trucks to grocery stores independent of the big food chains, to bakeries with deli counters and to taverns with sandwich menus. He liked gossiping with butchers and bartenders and talking the bakery girls out of a doughnut to go with his thermos of coffee. He thought of himself as a salesman rather than a truck driver, though he was both.

Some Christmases he gave his grownup nephews Albert and Dave wieners in twenty-four-pound cartons or a ten-pound salami—their choice. They always picked the salami, and when they said, "Thanks, Uncle Bozo," he would say, "Don't mention it—you've got an uncle in the business." This was Bozo's idea of a joke. It wasn't, of course, very funny, but if either Albert or Dave caught on that they were supposed to laugh, Bozo would laugh till he cried, and his hen's comb fell down over his forehead. If neither laughed, he didn't. It wasn't a joke then. Bozo was pliable that way. In proof of this, he thought of Albert and Dave as his own sons. His son Freddy wasn't really his.

Bozo's wife Virginia was considered a beauty when she was sixteen and they eloped. They lied about her age and married on his way to boot camp in Missouri. Bozo never had more than two things to say about Missouri: "I didn't see a mule there," and "It was so hot it made your ass sweat."

Albert and Dave were babies then, children of Bozo's only brother, who was older by ten years and so, out of the war.

Somewhere in a box of his war memorabilia is a picture of Bozo and Virginia with their marriage witnesses, two strangers hired for five bucks each by a Kansas City justice-of-the-peace whose wife played the accordion and took one snapshot for an extra five. Bozo inclines his head toward Virginia's shoulder and seems about to rest it there. They are at this time exactly the same height. Her auburn hair half beards his chin in broad, open curls. She stands erect, artificially dignified, holding her gardenia nosegay, and seeming determined to compensate for this ceremony's tackiness.

Virginia is from a good family whose fortune was made in rock quarries among red and gray granite for tombstones and the facades of public buildings. Their witnesses are a plump, matron imitation in a print housedress and a besotted derelict who perhaps has left his soup cooling on the justice's back doorstep.

From boot camp, leaving train fare home for Virginia, Bozo went overseas to the Saar Valley, Luxembourg, Freiberg, and finally to Czechoslovakia after the war ended. There in the central square of a small town, he saw from a moving jeep the bronze statue of a man standing ten feet high above the Bosso family name, unlopped and uncorrupted.

With her train fare home, Virginia moved to St. Louis instead and rented a room in a house called "Waiting Women of the War." She worked in the Brown Company shoe factory, manufacturing army boots, and evaded her family's attempts to find her. A year later she moved to Newark where Bozo had shipped from Pier 87. Virginia had lovers while Bozo was away, and she grew four inches.

Afterwards they were re-united (as they say in all such stories), went home together with the Iron Curtain descending over the Bosso homeland, and were properly married in keeping with the status of Virginia's family.

In an album is a picture of this wedding. Virginia, before an altar, is attended by a high school friend and an older sister, Bozo by his brother and Virginia's older brother. All of Virginia's people are tall and seem buttressed by granite. Bozo's brother and Bozo himself—despite his army uniform worn for the pleasure of his bride's family—look like hapless gypsies who have just crashed a society function and are about to be thrown out. Behind the wedding group, in the fashion of the day, hangs the crucified Christ with bloodied side. Of his two weddings, Bozo preferred that with the unknown derelict as his best man.

He had a Purple Heart for one gimpy leg, and the G. I. Bill. He refused help from Virginia's family and went to work for a sausage company driving a truck on a circuit through a new sales territory. He sold pickle loaf, variously-spiced salami, and the first skinless wieners to small businesses on a hundred-mile route. Three days a week he was on the road. Until business expanded, he worked the other two days and Saturday mornings in the sausage plant.

Two weeks after their second wedding and four weeks after they were re-united, Virginia revealed her midterm pregnancy. Bozo lurched out into the front yard of a house they were renting. This was in late spring. From beds flanking their walkway, peonies already drooped their pink and white globes. Virginia followed him and stood cautiously behind him to one side, one foot on the sidewalk and the other on the lawn as if contemplating a quick getaway. Their backs were to their Cape Cod with its white siding and blue shutters. Staring ahead out into the street where a boy on a bicycle and a neighborhood mail delivery van whizzed by, they adopted at first the deliberately muted voices of shy couples in public places.

Virginia, however, was not shy, having her family's habit of blunt assertiveness. She could also think on her feet, as a certain kind of glibness in tough circumstances is described.

"I'm sorry—I really am," she said.

"Listen here," Bozo said. He was anything but glib. His was a frail colloquialism—*listen here*—a preface to something too emotional for words, and just then he had no further words.

Virginia, on the other hand felt talkative. "We weren't really married. I lied about my age to get a license, and it could have been overturned."

Bozo saw black ants toiling among the peony globes. He also saw that Virginia's argument was illogical, irrelevant, and self-serving, but rebuttal didn't appeal to him.

"We weren't really married," Virginia repeated with both feet on the sidewalk now. Her voice had grown airy and informative. "And it was the same with you as with anyone else I might have been with." Her thoughts here concluded elsewhere than she intended, so she quickly amended them. "No, not the same—awful. I only meant that in the eyes of the law it was all the same." She lied here in consideration of his pride.

Bozo's pride was past consideration. "In the eyes of the law," he mocked. He pranced around her in ridiculous, elfish poses, exploding. "Marriage overturned?" he whined.

He tripped in the middle of a jig, toppled over, and sprawled on the grass at her feet. She towered above him against a background of white clouds with tops like cauliflowers. The mail delivery van drove back down the street, slowing while its driver squinted. A neighbor across the street was beckoning his wife to their living room window.

From the grass, Bozo shouted up, "And you grew so tall from all that screwing you took!" His feet had fallen into a peony bush, tangled with pink globes while his arms tangled with white. Virginia seemed to shudder. He left her alone standing in the front yard.

He drove out on his sales route and stayed a whole week. When he was a hundred and fifty miles away and one day overdue at the sausage plant, he phoned his boss and said he was trying to open up a new sales territory. He was, in fact, in a hotel in Rochester, with his truck parked in an alley behind, its refrigeration unit broken, and his wieners rotting.

"Get back here tomorrow, and I won't fire you," his boss said. "Your father-in-law has called here three times asking for you. You can't go out on your own like this. It's my business, not yours. What the hell's wrong, anyway?"

Bozo excused himself and hung up. He left his hotel room, and instead of taking the elevator, which was standing open on his floor, he walked four flights down to the hotel bar. It was late afternoon, and the bar was filled with suits and ties. Behind a lavender tie stood someone he recognized from his platoon in Czechoslovakia, a sergeant named Wilkin whom he had known but slightly.

For Wilkin, however, this was like a chance encounter of best friends. "For Christ's sake, it's a small world," he said, oozing fellowship. His voice quivered since this was his second bar stop of the late afternoon. Wilkin sold insurance these days. He had walked in with three or four others in suit coats, but mounted the stool alongside Bozo and draped a limp arm over his shoulder.

"Well, I'll be..." he said whenever their conversation lagged during the hour or so they sat there together. Each time the bartender brought them another round, Wilkin put his arm back over Bozo's shoulder, and kept his other resting in his lap out of sight beneath the bar. Wilkin appeared to be preoccupied at these times, as if mentally perusing actuarial tables, and so with two hands free, Bozo bought each round, even though he knew the trick. Since he already felt like a sucker, at least he didn't have to pretend.

Sergeant Wilkin wore a peach-colored sport jacket, which seemed to have folded papers sticking out of all its pockets. His lavender tie, loosened, dangled beneath an open shirt collar and a double chin. At first, they talked about the war and the life insurance business.

"The need for insurance is ever-present," Wilkin believed. "We never know how near." As though he were revealing company secrets, he slurred this in Bozo's ear. His tone was ominously low, his breath part bubble gum and part cigar smoke. Since Bozo himself was drinking, he couldn't smell Wilkin's whiskey.

"Death..." Wilkin continued. Since his voice was beyond control, death emerged as a loud, one-syllable laugh echoing along the bar, followed by a hiccup. On either side of them, men stopped talking and stared into their drinks. "Death waits around some corner up ahead," was

Wilkin's view, his voice temporarily under control once more. He lightly elbowed Bozo. "Old soldiers like us needn't call it *passing away*, I hope." Bozo shook his head, though he wasn't sure what he wanted to call it. "Death, like the need for insurance, is ever-present," said Wilkin.

They both agreed that however close such things might be, the war seemed far away now and their reunion occurring in some distant future where they were surprised to find themselves. They spoke of it that way—as if twenty years had elapsed, instead of barely one—and soon aided by this feeling and a half dozen whiskey-sevens, Bozo was able to see even his troubles with Virginia as receding into this same artificial distance like a painted stage set where difficult facts played themselves out and became bearable.

"You haven't changed a bit," Wilkin said at one point. He fingered a sheaf of insurance papers in his right coat pocket. "I'm into both whole life and term."

"I have my G.I. life insurance," said Bozo, heading off the pitch he saw coming.

"You need more than that—that's barely enough to plant you in the ground," said the sergeant, pointing to the floor beneath their barstools as if they sat upon the very spot where Bozo would one day rest in peace.

They faced a bar mirror where they addressed their own reflections above a line of whiskey bottles from which they appeared to look back at themselves over the top of an irregular fence. Later, when he was thoroughly drunk and had spent another ten dollars on Wilkin, Bozo blurted out the story of Virginia. In the bar mirror his chin seemed impaled on a bottle of Jack Daniels.

"My wife screwed around behind my back," he said. "She's four inches taller. She's pregnant."

Wilkin had discovered that the room was spinning. Minutes before, he had upended his whiskey and soda and sent the bartender leaping for a rag, but with Bozo's revelation he appeared to sober up. He spread a pudgy hand out before him palm down on the bar and counted his fingers.

"That's really tough to take. I never heard anything like it before," he said. He tapped his fingers on the bar—one, two, three, four—spread them as far apart as they would go, closed them again as if he measured distances. He pivoted on his stool and spoke directly to Bozo. "Does that mean she's taller than you now? —I'm also into family life...."

Wilkin's voice wavered, then slid away into a

long, gurgling slur. He passed out, falling over the bar with his measuring hand under his face and his free arm dangling at his side. The bartender leaped for his rag again.

Bozo left him there, took the elevator upstairs to his room, and fell asleep crossways on his bed with his clothes on. He awoke in the middle of the night with bedspread ribbing in red furrows across his face. He drove his truck home. Along the way, he threw his rotten wieners in the ditch. At daybreak, he arrived with the sausage plant just opening.

"Stay right here," his boss said.

Here was a ramshackle room adjacent to the boss's office. Through the fiberboard wall separating them, Bozo overheard his boss on the phone—though not precisely what he was saying. The boss walked into the ramshackle room.

"Stay here," he said again. "Have a cup of coffee." He pointed to an enamel pot on a hot plate atop a card table in a corner beneath a stained and curling railroad calendar. While Bozo poured himself a cup, he studied the calendar as if trying to discern what the future might offer. *May* was the month in view, and this was middle June. In May's picture a bright red passenger train was about to enter a mountain tunnel.

Upslope from the train on a basalt promontory, mountain goats, a ram and three ewes peered down.

The coffee tasted warmed-over from yesterday if not last month, but Bozo sipped it anyway, rubbing his forehead between sips, trying to free himself from a hangover headache throbbing over his right eye and occasionally down into it with a stabbing pain. He was alone with his thoughts about last month for fifteen minutes before the door opened. The six-foot-four quarried frame of his father-in-law confronted him.

"Ten thousand dollars," his father-in-law said after an exchange of greetings and significant glances, "and a better job than you'll ever have here."

He straddled a wooden chair backward with his broad front dwarfing its spindled back. Even sitting down, he towered over Bozo, though for all his imposing size, Virginia's father didn't look healthy, and like everything else about him, the signs of his ailments were large: large puffs under his eyes, large wrinkles under his ears, a gagging cough convulsing his chest.

"I don't want your money. I don't want your job," Bozo replied.

"I respect your pride, your desire to make it

on your own." He was stopped by a fit of coughing. His voice shook.

"Listen here," Bozo said. A disdainful thought might have followed, but he let it go while he waited through his father-in-law's next coughing fit. He felt a pain in his eye where last night's whiskey still festered. His hen's comb, already drooping this morning, now seemed utterly lifeless, a rag hanging on the wet basin of his sweaty forehead. "There's no use talking about this," he said at last, when there was silence again in the room. "I've made up my mind to go back to Virginia anyway, and I don't want your help to do it." He stared into an inch of black coffee in his cup, his reflected eye gleaming onyx there. His father-in-law suddenly relaxed and slouched like an overcoat over the back of his chair. "I won't be bribed," Bozo said.

"This is your pride talking," his father-in-law said indifferently. "I don't bribe anyone." Besides he had gotten what he came for.

"I don't want anything," Bozo said.

His father-in-law shrugged.

"Because maybe it's just as a fellow tried telling me last night—other things could be more important." Bozo wasn't thinking of Sergeant Wilkin's life insurance.

"Exactly," his father-in-law said. "We've got to consider more important things—appearances, for example." He lowered his voice and cleared his throat of what sounded like a tremendous clot of phlegm. "Virginia told us the kid isn't yours. Who can blame you for being upset?" He reached for the coffee pot. "Still we have to think of appearances...."

Bozo winced. "It tastes like burnt shit," he said, describing both the coffee and his personal circumstances.

Sometimes everybody is right, though perhaps not in the way they meant to be, and an instance of this was Bozo and Virginia's father in their opinions about her pregnancy. Both of them correctly surmised that other things would prove more important, but the most important other thing was neither the family's public image, which it was the impulse of Virginia's father to protect, nor was it the dimly conceived notion of honoring commitments, which was Bozo's life-long impulse to practice. What ultimately proved most important was the cough that kept interrupting their conversation this day, for when it finally got the better of Virginia's father, she would inherit a million dollars Bozo didn't want.

Long before this was clear, the baby was born,

and Bozo named him, first name and last, the selection of his first name a peace offering from Virginia and the last name a necessity they both took for granted without discussing it. Frederick Bosso the baby was called. Bozo didn't even have to adopt him. He just showed up at the hospital and did his best to look like the proud father.

He liked the name Frederick because it had, he thought, a noble European smack, fitting in a family for whom bronze statues had been erected in public squares. Virginia, slightly reneging on her peace offering, called the boy Freddy, which Bozo disliked intensely. This merely fired Virginia's resolve so that the nickname in her usage acquired an incongruously formal, high-brow ring, overreaching even Frederick.

Often Bozo wondered about the uncorrupted family name he had seen at the foot of a statue in Czechoslovakia, and when he had drunk much of the beer he had begun preferring to whiskey, he would sometimes speak of changing Bosso back to its original. He would speak of this most passionately to anyone who might listen, but rarely either to his brother or Virginia, both of whom thought the idea ridiculous.

His nephews Albert and Dave, on the other hand, were young enough to take a romantic view of family history. They encouraged Bozo's fabricated tale of his Czech merchant great grandfather who carted his money to the bank in wheelbarrows, saving his town from bankruptcy, which in turn showed its gratitude by erecting a statue in his honor. It became a great ball of yarn wound from the flimsiest of threads. Bozo's brother heard of this and complained.

"Keep your foolish notions out of my kids' heads," he warned him. "Christ, they're starting to write in their school books that long, stupid name nobody can spell. We're all Americans, so who gives a damn about statues? What's past is past. Leave it alone, Eugene."

"I changed my name once for you," Virginia said. "I won't do that again. If you're so hot about your family's money, what's wrong with my father's?"

But Bozo couldn't leave it alone, as his brother advised, nor would he accept from Virginia's family a gift larger than he could buy them in return. He quit discussing family history with his nephews—at least while they still lived at home—but butchers and tavern keepers on his sales route kept hearing about it.

He prowled the house he built for Freddy and Virginia in search of valuables she might have accepted from her family, anything resembling a bribe. Since Virginia was cautious and her family mindful of Bozo's pride, he seldom found much to fight about.

Bozo was kind to Freddy but inevitably distant. So well kept was the family secret, he often heard from friends the small talk of how his son resembled him. He made unintelligible responses and burrowed more deeply into a family history he hoped would reveal a connection to that part of Czechoslovakia where the bronze statue stood.

He had letters in languages he couldn't read from foreign archivists and government clerks whose names he couldn't pronounce. The upshot of it all dismayed him, for family blood in Europe kept running south into the frontiers of the old Ottoman Empire. He thought the error lay in his research and in his never quite trying to hoist into his family tree the statue taller than Virginia's father, who was now dying and leaving her a fortune.

"Your family money is an embarrassment to me," Bozo said. "We have always made it on our own."

"Your pride is an embarrassment to me," Virginia said at the end of a long argument. "It's my money, and I won't throw it away just to make you feel taller. You've been good to me about lots of things, but about this, you're nuts."

She filed for divorce within a month of her father's death, moving away with Freddy and her inheritance.

Both of them Bozo missed. He had lived with Virginia and Freddy for eleven years, but he didn't contest the divorce. He even understood why she would want to have her money, but he was happy that it wasn't his as well.

These days he was driving his meat truck five days a week to forty small towns. He didn't work Saturdays anymore. His inventory included a dozen kinds of sausages and three-dozen kinds of cold cuts.

He sold the house Virginia had abandoned to him and moved into a small apartment near the sausage plant. From Virginia, he only heard once further, that indirectly. She was changing Freddy's name to her second husband's. A lawyer met with him in the ramshackle room at the sausage plant. He needed a sworn statement and signed papers. Bozo swore and signed as directed. He was still pliable. The arrangements seemed fair to him, but the lawyer appeared to want a fight.

"The child isn't really mine," Bozo told him.

"That hasn't come up in the litigation," the

lawyer said. "In the eyes of the law, you are signing away one of your most important claims in life. Do you understand the significance of that?"

"He wasn't really mine," Bozo said. "She once said that in the eyes of the law we weren't really married either."

"I don't know anything about that—it hasn't come up," the lawyer said.

Bozo signed the last of the papers without reading them. Witnesses were his boss and two guys from the sausage store which had recently opened on plant premises. When the lawyer tried to speak further, he waved him off.

He went over to his brother's house after work and helped Albert and Dave restore a motorcycle they had bought from a junk dealer. It had been in an accident. It smoked and leaked oil. Its wheels wobbled hopelessly. Bozo junked it again, and bought a pair of new ones for his nephews.

By the time Albert and Dave married, a year or so apart, Bozo had developed serious health problems. He was given an honored place in both their weddings. Dave, in a toast, said you couldn't have a better uncle than Bozo had been. In colored pictures of the groom's family, he looks green. His heart was enlarging: a metaphor about him was becoming literal. He had become a big-hearted man.

He gave up smoking and beer. He dieted and took pills of three colors. He quit his sausage route and spent months in Veteran's hospitals between short trips home. His condition was terminal unless he got a transplant. He took his name off the waiting list.

Albert and Dave were close. They even built houses across an alley from one another, in a suburban development across the river and upstream from Bozo's sausage plant. On the corner of their block had once been a tavern—now remodeled into a house—where Bozo had delivered boiled ham and beer salami every Friday morning in the old days when Albert and Dave's street was a narrow, tar road between farms.

Because their wives didn't get along, Albert and Dave would meet in the alley behind their houses. A month before Bozo died, they were standing there between Albert's two-car garage and Dave's privet hedge. Smoking and drinking beer from cans, they talked at first of Albert's trip to Europe. He was a chemical engineer and had just returned from three months of work there.

"Uncle Bozo wanted me to check out the

family statue for him," he said. "He wrote a lot of letters trying to find out more about it himself, but nobody knew what he was talking about, I guess."

"He's still nuts about his name," Dave said. "I saw him last week in the hospital. He said he should never have let Virginia change that kid of hers name."

"He's dying now, and he never even got around to changing his own back to the original."

They were both struck by the melancholy of that thought, and fell silent for a while. Dave brought out two more cans of beer from a cooler stored in the shade under his hedge. This was late summer, with the sun high but the air cool, and small birds were hopping about among the hedge berries.

"I had all kinds of problems and didn't get into Czechoslovakia till my last week there," Albert said. "I would have given up on the whole project, but it's tough to let Uncle Bozo down." He opened his fresh can of beer, but didn't drink yet.

"You found the statue then?" Dave asked.

"I found it all right, exactly where he said it was, in a small, non-industrial town, mostly a market center for farmers—it can't have changed much since Bozo was there. And just as he says, there's a statue in its only square with every main street in town running right up to it, but you know what? He was wrong, damn it all, Dave, completely wrong. The name under it isn't anything like our old name, or even our name the way we spell it now, not close. What do you think of that?"

"Maybe the Communists changed it," Dave suggested.

"Hell no—I thought about that too. I checked around, and the statue's been there for a hundred and fifty years with pigeons shitting on it. Nothing's changed. He looked at it and saw a vision, you might say. No wonder nobody over there knew what he was talking about."

"Bozo always wanted to be important—you're not going to tell him, are you?"

Albert shook his head and took a first sip of his beer. He dislodged a stone with the toe of his shoe and scuffed it down the alley. "It would kill him sooner than his heart," he said.

"God damn it," Dave said. "He built his whole life around it, and it was just a mirage."

A wind stirred along the alley and swirled into the privet hedge where it blew the small brown birds away. Albert opened a door of his double garage, and they sat inside, finishing their beer on a plank between sawhorses. Like almost all garages, even old ones made of stone, Albert's smelled of new wood.

Dave told a story about Bozo that he had kept to himself from the day of Albert's wedding. Bozo had been drinking beer and talking a lot. He wasn't supposed to be drinking beer, though, so when his can was stolen from the table by one of a half-dozen little kids hanging around, Dave noticed but didn't say anything. Bozo in animated conversation lit a cigarette he wasn't supposed to smoke and didn't miss his beer. Five minutes later when he reached for it, the surprise was Dave's. It was back on the table at his elbow.

"Later on, I got this story from your wife's niece," Dave said. "They were mostly your wife's family, those little kids, I think, and this girl was a tattler who came to me with her story. It seems that one of the boys ran with Bozo's beer can downstairs into the bathroom. All the kids had been in and out of there and not flushing the toilet. He tossed it in the stool, and it filled up. Then another kid, figuring to keep everyone out of trouble, pulled it out and brought it back upstairs to the table."

"And Bozo drank it?" Albert asked.

"The whole damn thing without saying a word about it."

"Jesus," Albert said.

"Who knew?" Dave said.

"Damn kids," Albert said.

"Bozo always liked kids, even Freddy," Dave said. "He was the most generous man I ever met, but he had this awful passion about being somebody and not accepting help." Though Bozo lived yet, their talk about him had fallen into the past tense, which made him sound dead. Neither of them bothered to correct the impression. "He might even have laughed off drinking a can of piss, but I didn't want him to tell him."

"He drank the whole can," Albert said, finishing his. "Jesus, it's funny and it's awful."

"I know what you mean. That's why your news about the statue made me think of it now—it's so much like Bozo's whole life."

"It's funny and it's awful," Albert said again.

HOMECOMING AT HOLE-IN-THE-DAY

*P*eter's youngest son Bernard came by Greyhound Bus from a distant town where he lived with his mother still. Doug, between college terms, was finishing the second week of a visit he'd told his dad would be only one week this summer. Tony, Peter's oldest, promised to arrive by sunset if the late summer weekend traffic didn't slow his trip from the national park where he worked. Peter Forester was thinking of this gathering of his sons as a homecoming, though only he would have regarded it that way, for none of his sons had ever really lived here. They had grown up with their mother and had infrequently been with Peter, and seldom all of them together.

In his small house on the shore of Lake Hole-in-the-Day (named for an Indian chief born during an eclipse of the sun), Peter hadn't room for a family gathering, in fact. He planned to sleep outside with Bernard, leaving his only bedroom for Tony, who camped for a living and let his dad know he was tired of it. Doug would take the couch. When they all left him the next afternoon, and when Peter once more slept alone in his house, the summer would be over by his reckoning, one week short of Labor Day.

There was no denying the evidence of blue wild asters and goldenrod blooming in the wooded border of his property where a lawnmower wouldn't go, nor that a neighbor's woodpile had been neatly stacked into ricks. Winter would come on, even if warm days ahead belied the intuition.

As certain as he could be of all such things, present and somewhere up ahead of him, he had no way of knowing when he might have all his sons together again. He sensed it might be a very long time.

Whimsically, in honor of the occasion, Peter had tried to fly a flag. The rigging above him wound up in a hopeless tangle, the result of a pulley working its rusty mischief. The flag stuck seven feet from the top of an iron pole that was much inclined to sway with tugs far less insistent than his became.

Giving up at last and stepping out from a lilac bush that had grown around the pole, he said, "At least it's higher than half-mast."

Bernard stood by with his hair in his eyes, his usual lopsided smile, and his ignorance of his father's more abstract concerns. Since he couldn't think of anything to say about the flag, Bernard plucked a leaf from the bush and absently tore it in half along its central vein. His father's hand upon his forehead brushed the hair from his eyes with equal absence.

"We've the only flag that I know of on this side of the lake," Peter said, "and I don't fly it half enough."

In fact, he never flew his flag, even on holidays, which this was not—except in a personal sense—and so, from disuse, its rigging had deteriorated.

Bernard plucked another leaf and gazed up at the old flag with its closet wrinkles and its two stars less than fifty. He sensed that his father wanted him to say something about it.

It unfurled in an easterly breeze with what might have seemed a mare's-tail bunting above it.

Westward, a cirrus haze diffused but did not much dim the sunlight. While Bernard tore asunder a third leaf, his father admired, without interpreting, these signs of tomorrow's rain.

"The gas station out on the highway has a flagpole," Bernard said at last. His bus had left him beneath it just this morning. This wasn't quite what he wanted to say.

An annoyance to think of that, his father's face suggested. Nor would such a flag really count since the gas station wasn't on the lake.

Peter stepped back into the lilac bush to give the halyard another tug. With the pole swaying in a wide arc, Bernard tried to redeem himself by offering to climb it.

"You'd break your neck," his father said. "We'll have to leave it as it is." If it wasn't quite the token of celebration he wished, neither was it quite a sign of grief.

Their attention was drawn toward a splash from the boat dock and then laughter. Doug was swimming with Barbara, a neighbor girl, giving Bernard an opportunity to slip away and unpack a tent borrowed from Barbara's parents.

Peter settled down to watch them all from a picnic table in the shade of three birch clumps whose shadows were lengthening already in the direction of his beach. Here, with sunset at their backs and their feet tucked under them in the sand, foregoing even the picnic table, they would eat when Tony got home. He had in the refrigerator a potato salad of his own creation, a canned ham, and a casserole of baked beans provided by Barbara's mother.

At the end of the dock, Doug gracefully heaved himself out of the water and flopped belly down upon the planking. Barbara followed, adjusted her swimming suit around her breasts, and sat beside him with a towel folded over her brown shoulders and her hand on his back. She was dark and attractive and on the zany side as truly lighthearted girls come across. Peter could only suppose that on her account his middle son had arrived a week early and stayed with him two weeks instead of one.

"We'll put up the center section first," he shouted to Bernard, "and then the sides."

He knew nothing of tents, but that's what Barbara told him of her family's red tent. Bernard waved from a clutter of fiberglass piping. A tent flap fluttered in his face. Up the beach came Doug and Barbara to help him. Peter shouted that a red tent reminded him of carnivals, and Bernard waved again. What a holiday for flag-flying it was to have all one's children home!

Barbara gave directions, pointing with one hand while with the other holding her long wet hair from her face. A shape emerged from a floppy heap where only a moment before Bernard had sprawled laughing, triangular at first and then with the sides setting up, an elongated scarlet W which blocked Peter's view of his boat dock and sections of beach either side of it. For an instant among the billowing red nylon, the shouts and gestures and stray cords untangling in the breeze, he had seen the hands of Doug and Barbara brush and clasp. He stood up from the picnic table and joined them all in front of the tent.

Barbara giggling asked him, "Are you sure you want to sleep here?"

"Like a rock I will," he said. He looked forward to camping with Bernard. They'd never done that before, and it seemed to him the sort of thing fathers and sons should do at least once.

"It'll be more like sleeping on a rock," Doug suggested. "Give me the couch anytime." He pushed his brother through the tent's open door, and Bernard lay down inside and pretended to snore. Again, the hands of Doug and Barbara brushed. Bernard sat up, grimacing and pretending to rub his back.

Sunset came but Tony didn't. Birch shadows died upon tent and beach. Peter peeled the tin cover from his ham and decided to eat without him. The breeze had freshened into a wind off the lake with a sharp chill and the smell of algae in it.

Doug ate hurriedly and spoke into his plate where a thick ham slice separated his father's potato salad from the neighbor's beans.

"It's going to be cold for you two out in that tent tonight—maybe I should sleep out there instead." He wore a blue sweatsuit over his swimming trunks, with the loose cords of its hood dangling above his plate. Doug had a habit of not looking at people as he spoke to them and then stealing glances when their attention seemed elsewhere.

Peter's eyes darted elsewhere, then back in time to catch his son's. He chose to regard his son as shy rather than illusive, but which it really was, he didn't know. He hadn't been with any of his sons enough to think he knew them very well, and Doug kept to himself much more than the other two, so even a couple of weeks hadn't yielded much.

Peter had a better understanding of Barbara, the neighbor girl, her parents, their dog, even the local mail delivery guy. He looked up from his plate again, through a window facing him at the lake whose whitecaps foamed amber as the sun set.

"Where the hell is Tony?" he said.

"Probably at a bar," Bernard suggested. Doug kicked him under the table. "I don't want any beans," Bernard said, pushing aside the bowl Doug slid his way, "and what are you kicking me for?"

"Eat them anyway," Doug said. "Barbara's mother had them in the oven all day."

Bernard stabbed his fork into the bowl and impaled three beans which he arranged in a triangle atop his ham slice. "Okay, because you're in love, *Dougie,* I'll eat beans."

"Shut up, and don't call me Dougie."

Bernard displayed his lopsided smile. "Barbara does," he said.

"Shut up, *Bernie,*" Doug said. "That's different —she doesn't mean what you mean by it."

"What *does* she mean by it?"

"I wonder what's keeping Tony," Peter said arching an eyebrow over their argument.

"Heavy traffic," Doug suggested. "Tourists."

Peter knew it wasn't the parade of vacationers out on the highway that delayed his son. He had already eliminated that possibility by walking out to the highway while Doug and Bernard had finished staking the tent. It was nearly as empty as the evening sky. Not even a car at the gas station. In front of it an attendant sat in a lawn chair reading a comic book. Barbara's brother. Centered in a semicircle of lawn formed by the station's driveway was the flagpole Peter had never noticed.

Walking home, he had heard a loon crying from the lake. This primitive, cacophonous hoot accompanying the passing of days was not in itself unusual, but tonight it struck him that the sound of it wasn't grief and wasn't joy, but something in between and oddly purer for being so.

Doug pushed himself back from the table, finished eating first. "I'll see if I can borrow some extra blankets from Barbara's folks," he said. "You're going to need them out in the tent tonight, and I'm heading over there right now anyway."

"We've bothered them enough this weekend," Peter said. "Forget the blankets and stick around, so when Tony comes, we'll all be together. I'll light the fireplace. Everybody's leaving to-morrow already—it's our only chance to be together."

"Yeah," Doug said as though it didn't matter much to him. "I'll be back as soon as Tony shows up—you can count on it. And with blankets to throw over your sleeping bags."

"What's the rush? Have more ham," Peter called after him.

"No room for it—great ham though, great beans," Doug shouted from the other side of the screen door above which several moths fluttered around a porch light. On his way through the yard to Barbara's, he shoved the flagpole sending it crazily asway in an erratic arc with flag and halyard wrapping it.

"He's in love," Bernard declared.

"My old man's in a tizzy over Tony—I thought I'd never get out of there," Doug said to Barbara who waited for him by her father's firewood ricks, just beyond the illuminated circle of a yard light. And since she had waited long, she held in her hand as a token of her restlessness a bouquet of asters with broken stems.

"I hope the hell not," Peter was just saying to Bernard. "Doug's too young to be in love. And forget the beans if you don't want any."

"Doug is twenty," Bernard said. "I'm thirteen. I ate three beans. Mom says we're all men now."

By midnight, an overcast sliding eastward at last hid every star and circled in halo the gibbous moon just then rising. Tony still hadn't arrived. Doug was next door yet, and Peter and Bernard bedded down in the red tent after sitting for a while in front of the fireplace. Since the tent effectively cut off the wind, it was warmer inside than they expected, even without the extra blankets Doug had forgotten to bring. For a time, Bernard lay half out of his sleeping bag, leaning first on one arm and then the other, listening to a radio. Peter had brought along in his jacket pocket a deck of cards, and they played "Crazy-Eights" till Bernard remarked that the game, once his favorite, now seemed juvenile.

"Sorry," said Peter, "I guess I'm not keeping up with you guys —you're all growing up so fast."

It seemed anything but fast to Bernard, but he didn't say so and instead said, "No big deal," which seemed to stand for all of it—for growing up, for his father's not keeping up, and for playing juvenile games.

Between them burned a battery-powered lamp atop a step stool from Peter's kitchen. It lit up the center of their tent with a ruddy, warm glow reflecting off its nylon fabric. Around them faintly in their clothing was the cinnamon aroma of birch wood smoke they had brought with them from sitting by the fireplace.

Peter curled silently down into his sleeping bag, listening to Bernard's radio until Bernard turned it off and slept, it seemed, and then in the dark with the battery lamp also off he listened to his son's breathing settled into a rhythm with that of the lake waves behind them slapping against the boat, and then the boat knocking against the dock, then water sliding upon the sand. Here, too, were the sounds of wind through leaves and a loon disturbed somewhere once and also a bird from its roost up over their tent with a single chirp. A cricket under the porch. Peter sorted through all this, searching for the sounds of Tony coming home. He didn't find them. He couldn't sleep. He crept from the tent for a walk along the lake.

In what had become a very dark evening, he groped his way down the beach, navigating as much by sounds and the feeling of sand beneath his bare feet as by the feeble illumination of distant shore lights flickering like substitute starlight. Behind him, turning the sand there light gray with darker tree shadows falling into it, was a single pale slash cast lakeward from his porch light. Ahead of him was another such from an upstairs window of the neighbor's house. He sat on the beach halfway between these and fifty feet or so from what he took to be an overturned rowboat, its bow upon the upper beach and its stern concealed beneath a tree.

He faced into the east wind with its damp chill and its vegetable fragrances of lake life. He hunched over with his knees doubled up in front of him, his arms locked over his knees, and his chin nestled in the hollow formed there. Though it was a position suggesting thoughtfulness, he no longer had any thoughts. If he seemed to brood, he didn't brood. The pose kept him warm at least. Almost dozing after a while, unmindful of his surroundings, he was startled by a sudden movement to his right.

Out of the overturned rowboat and for an instant into light suddenly brilliant shot the white legs of Barbara. As quickly they withdrew again into what he now recognized as a mound of blankets and not a boat at all. Doug and Barbara were making love. Peter winced and looked away. A car door slammed. Another movement in the blankets.

"God, it's Tony!" he heard Doug say.

Peter dodged out of the crossfire of lights from Tony's car flashing through the trees. Behind him the overturned boat had moved into deeper shadows. A screen door slammed. Tony's car, parked barely a foot from the porch, was empty when he got to it. He reached through its open window and snapped off its headlights. He smelled gin. Tony had gone into the house and collapsed across his father's bed. In the living room was Bernard, sitting cross-legged on the floor, gazing into the fireplace where a few birch embers glowed.

"He's drunk," Bernard said as his father walked by him with the battery lamp in hand. "Tony is royally stewed."

Peter tried rousing him. Tony rolled over and groaned, blowing an oily plume of gin aroma into his father's face. He shielded his eyes from the battery lamp, opened his mouth a time or two without saying anything, and fell back to sleep.

"I'd let him sleep—he's so stewed," Bernard said from the living room.

Where the hell did Bernard pick up a word like *stewed*, he wondered? No one under the age of fifty used it anymore. Not for the first time he felt that he knew nothing about his sons. Tony drank, Doug screwed around, Bernard used old words.

Peter closed the bedroom door, tiptoeing out as if quiet were necessary, as if Tony might awaken and begin to make sense, as if his own bare feet were noisy. "I didn't know Tony drank," he whispered.

"Tony? Dad, Tony likes to booze it up. I figured that's what he was doing tonight—you should see him sometimes."

"Booze it up, you said?"

"Yeah," said Bernard.

"I'll have a talk with him in the morning," Peter said.

"Mom's already tried that," said Bernard, "a hundred times."

On their way back to the tent they met Doug with a bundle of blankets in his arms.

"Tony's stewed again," Bernard said to Doug.

"No kidding," Doug said. Nonchalantly he handed the blankets to his father. They were sandy and smelled of perfume. Peter winced again.

"Good night," Doug said "—it's the couch for me." As he stepped onto the porch, a bird chirped, then fell silent.

"Doug," Peter said.

"Yeah," Doug said. He turned around and looked down at his father over the porch rail.

Peter hesitated, searching through his mind where there seemed only words that wouldn't work, not any of the vulgarities one might call sex with a neighbor girl, being certain of nothing more obvious, not even the love one might hope to call it. Nothing seemed to fit tonight, and why, after all, did he find it so embarrassing, as if he himself had been caught? "Doug," he said, "turn off the porch light when you go in, will you?"

"Sure," Doug said.

"And I want to talk with you tomorrow."

"Sure," Doug said.

Falling from the blankets as Peter threw them to one side of their tent was a sprig of wild aster. Bernard leaned on his arm out of his sleeping bag.

"Well, we're all together at last," he said, smiling lopsided.

"Are we?" Peter said. His voice was shaky. He crawled into his sleeping bag.

Bernard turned off the battery light, but kept talking in the dark, recounting the events of the day in story outline form, leading up to Tony's appearance, Doug's reappearance, and their return to this tent. "It's so—we're all together," he concluded.

For a moment Peter felt his son's hand find his shoulder from the darkness beside him. Tentatively it touched him and then withdrew into the darkness again. This was enough. Peter slept.

At sunrise he awoke to the patter of rain on the red tent's roof, and mixed with it was the shrill sound of metal complaining. Bernard was gone. Through an open fold in the tent door which he'd left unzipped in leaving, Peter could see him high on the flagpole shimmying up with his pajama shirt in a wad under his armpits.

"Bernard," he shouted as he stumbled outside in the rain. "Bernard, you'll break your neck."

The pole, which Peter tried to steady, was pitching sharply and straining against its broken concrete mooring. Peter set his shoulder against it. Lilac branches scratched his arms. "Bernard, for God's sake, get down," he shouted.

With his legs twining around the pole and one hand holding him up, Bernard reached out for the dangling halyard and unhooked the flag. As it fell, he slid down the pole, leaped clear of the lilac bush, and landed on his feet with a backward stagger.

"I'm okay," said Bernard, breathless. "I knew I

could get it down for you—I've been thinking about it all night."

Peter gathered in the wet corners of his flag from the lilac bush where it had fallen. Rain wetted his hair. Water trickled down his forehead and into his eyes. His vision blurred for a moment, then cleared again. From the lake came a loon's sunrise cry, still neither happy nor sad but in between like a flag stuck seven feet from the top.

"I'm okay," Bernard had said, grinning lopsided as always, clearly proud of himself.

"So am I," Peter said. What he expected at best or feared the worst would never be as pure as this.

INDIAN PAINTBRUSH

*L*ast August, Sarah moved north from Minneapolis to live with him in the lakeshore cottage he rented.

"Poltergeists," was how she explained this to her friends Laura and Joan, the most facetious reply she could invent to beg off their hundredth last-ditch quiz, those specters who make a hubbub in the walls and set the chair to rocking without anyone in it.

"Worse than no answer at all. Worse than love," said Laura.

"Admit it, you don't really know what you're doing," said Joan. Already she had persuaded her not to move all her stuff out. She owned the house and wouldn't for six months rent Sarah's room.

Sarah closed her eyes and pretended to pray at the dining room table where the three of them sat for what the other two insisted wasn't their last breakfast together. Neither of them liked him a bit. No, Sarah, didn't know what she was doing, but she could mock their concerns for a few seconds with her fingers pointed at a ceiling fixture of imitation candles. Then to her breast one half of the prayer pose came, palm in. "Most definitely *mea maxima culpa,*" she said.

"Oh hell," said Laura, "I'd rather blame poltergeists."

"I'd rather get to work on time," said Joan. She stood up and slid her grapefruit half across to Sarah. "Eat this, you will need it. Write, phone, good luck, all those things."

She whirled away out of the house, and Laura, pleading that she was sloppy at goodbyes, went upstairs to her room across the hall from Sarah's. Alone at the long mahogany table then, Sarah sat gazing its length through a plaster archway to a latticed front-room window until a familiar blue car filled three of its lower panes, her ghost arriving.

At the other end of this day they paused beside the redwood cottage with her boxes and bags yet on its doorstep. Breathing deeply from their exertions and their excitement, they took a first view of the lake as tourists do. Nearby a squirrel seemed to scold them from a blown-down jack pine whose trunk pointed the direction his thoughts ran.

"A village is only a quarter mile across the lake from here, but five miles by road around. In winter we'll just walk over on the ice or skate and get there as soon as driving. We're far away from people or near—we can have it both ways."

She wasn't bothered by having heard him say such things before, not once but many times in assorted versions with always the flavor of rehearsal her friends so much disliked. He was the sort to mull, to think of things before he said them, then to mull and speak again, forgetting that he had already said them.

The scene around them, her first sight of her new home with him, sustained his various reports, not their accuracy, but their sentiment. The lake had been nearer or farther away at other times he described it. The cottage whose crumbling step she was about to test had been larger and newer. She even suspected, without caring, that this wasn't at all the place he had in mind when he first suggested their living together. Somehow buildings, embankments, shorelines and forests and roads had all been altered and finally replaced as he built up in her mind this view like a new landscape painted over an old.

She didn't care today. She confronted the lake with him. The sun at their backs thrust their twin shadows over the unmown yard grass, arched over in summer wind furrows, heavy-headed and going to seed. Somewhere out there before the shaggy pines began their march to the lake, their shadows merged.

"It helps so much to see it for yourself," she said to him. "I believed what you said about it, but it makes all the difference to actually be here."

"Together," he added, for he had moved here himself a month before this.

She hadn't been sure she would stay till the winter he spoke of just now, to walk with him across the frozen lake, so tentative had seemed their understanding of each other before this moment. Yet now she easily imagined herself bundled to the nose and trudging through the snow into the village with him and coming back across the frozen lake with parcels, happy though her feet grew numb. Wasn't that why she was coming here to live with him in the first place—because it was mostly so easy to imagine? His life and hers improving together, happiness in such solitude, the vanilla fragrance of pine trees. He alone fretted over details.

"When I am not around, you won't be that far from people, not really," he said, his apology too evident for both of them. She expected to be alone here much of the time at first. He planned to look for a new job, one that let him stay home nights. "We'll have a phone put in," he said for the fourth or fifth time this day.

"I'll be all right," she said. "I don't care. I don't mind waiting a while." She could just see Laura and Joan cringing, coiling into knots of disappointment with her. She groped for his hand beside her. She inhaled deeply and tried to recognize the aromas around them—of bedstraw in bloom, pine-needle mulch, of being all right and not worrying and never minding. "And as for you," she said, "think how you might settle down here and get your life together." She saw here good things for the man she thought he was: the lake, habitually reflective, blue between the swaying trunks of jack pines and the steadier trunks of oaks; the isolation of their home here in this northern forest; its obvious invitation to mull one's way to satisfactory conclusions. "It's all here if you want it," she said.

"Yes, I've thought so too." He stooped to pick up one of her bags again, fumbled in his pocket for the door key. Twice he pulled out nickels instead, while she stood by with a cardboard box and a straw hat atop it lifted into her face tickling her nose with its thatchy brim. Now it seemed such a ridiculous tourist prop, so transient that it mocked her, that she wished she had left it behind in her room. "I'll stay on the road just a few more weeks to get money ahead—wrong pocket, I guess." He pulled out the nickels again. He switched hands with her bag and found the key.

Less easily than their winter walk across the lake could she imagine him getting free from his present work, which was selling wallpaper to retailers in fifty small towns where people had more use for paint. He worked on commission only and was often broke.

The next morning already he would have to leave for his northern sales route, stopping off midway to visit his two kids from a busted marriage. He would be gone three days, then home for two with her, then gone for another three on what he called too glibly his southern swing. When things went well, he stayed in motels;

when not, he slept in his car. His success she could judge by the wrinkles in his coat, his tired man's pallor. This was his life these days, stopping off for visits tourist-fashion where, circumstances otherwise, he might have stayed. She tried to imagine this changing.

But his few weeks of work merely preluded another few. The phone arrived, installed by a workman with a red pliers stuck in a loop on his coverall leg. "Snug little place you have here," the workman said, standing up from a hole he had drilled in the wall and glancing around. She agreed. It was still easy to think so. After that she was called every night from one of his small painted towns.

"Are you all right?" he asked her every night.

"I'm fine," she answered every night, whether or not she felt that way, but still most nights it wasn't a lie. "How did it go today?"

"Okay," he always said. Convictionless, she thought, evasive.

Then to make their talk seem less rehearsed she offered him some morsel of her day. "A sailboat scooted along the other side. I would have thought it too windy. I saw a porcupine in our yard. His quills swayed, his eyes were red. I caught a ride into the village this afternoon to look for a job. Everyone says it's the wrong time of the year. They say I should check back in the spring when the tourists return."

"There aren't any winter jobs in this God-forsaken country," he said, "for you or for me."

She winced, so new to her was this analysis of his prospects. One night she said to him, "When I opened the back door, six yellow leaves blew in at my feet. I glued them to the window in a spray." If he might have seen his children recently, she asked about them.

Autumn. He came home with a gray and white kitten, a frail and weepy-eyed sort who stood trembling on the kitchen countertop when he took it from his coat pocket and set it before her.

"No, thank you," she said. "I won't go through that again," though cats were a fancy of hers. While growing up in the city, she had made docile pets of what seemed entire litters in foreshortened retrospect, but always they were run over or eaten by stray dogs in the alley, either of which now struck her as inevitable. He knew that she had given up on cats. He knew, moreover, that they provoked Joan's asthma.

His blue car in the driveway next morning between a tall spruce and the clotheslines seemed spectral and as likely as the mists to drift. From a window she watched him melting the gray frost with his fingers and pushing it in clots from his windshield. He was hours from having to drive away, but he had grown fidgety and feeling the need for evasion, tinkered where he didn't have to. On the lake, two hundred feet from their cottage, ducks gathered for the morning's migration. The kitten, having slept between them on the quilts all night, danced around the floor chasing a thread from her dressing gown hem.

"In an hour the sun would have melted the frost for you," she said when he came in.

He shrugged and blew on his red fingers. She measured coffee into an enamel pot, experienced a sense that the two of them had begun to measure their words with each other this way. He stooped near her and picked up the kitten.

"A cat will keep you company when I'm out on the road," he said. Rehearsed.

"You call me every night for company. I left my job and moved in here hoping you'd travel less."

"Soon," he said.

She couldn't imagine it at all. She lifted a potted fern from the kitchen table where they now sat waiting for their coffee to boil, and in the low sunlight of an east window pretended to inspect its fronds. Her face wore the shadow lines of these in the ruddy light. The shadows trembled.

"He is only a kitten yet," she said. He'll need shots with winter coming on, and food all the time—love as much as food even. It's too much when you're taken by surprise."

What she meant to say was not exactly this, for she had a way with animals, and shots and caring for them would never be beyond her. But her loneliness and his was more than a cat could remedy. Of this she meant to remind him in that roundabout way that shy people will use to talk of a pet or a baby to reveal themselves.

Their being together so seldom was becoming too much, the endless cycles of his trips north and south on a job he only talked of quitting because, of course (and this she understood definitely now), he couldn't really afford to quit. He would never be money enough ahead to buy himself a reprieve. His sincerity, which she still believed, could never affect these facts. She set the fern back upon the table. Lately, with winter so near, her hope shedding like leaves its substance, she thought of returning to her room in a house where cats weren't allowed.

"Do you think I'm only trying to make leaving

here more difficult for you?" he asked. He squinted at the sleeping kitten as if there on his lap lay some point too distant for him to see. "If you must move back with your friends, we can always do something with the cat."

She knew of men who put kittens in potato sacks with bricks and drowned them in the river. He wasn't that sort at least. They were arguing now. "What *would* we do with it?" she asked. "Do you think it's so easy to pick up something and love it and then let go of it?"

"You needn't put it in that light."

"Oh," she said. She slid the potted fern back to precisely where a water stain marked its former place on the table. "Oh, I refuse to be a bitch to make all of this any plainer for you." She left him to make the bed. She took her time.

Above the stove over the coffee pot a plume of steam extended toward the ceiling. He threw the kitten on the floor and poured himself a cup. He drank half of it. He nibbled at a roll, shouting to her over his shoulder with crumbs on his lips. "I've got things to do before the morning gets away from us."

The sunlight, she noted looking after him, was still between rather than above the trees. What was getting away from them was not the morning.

Out on the lake knocking against its tree-stump mooring was an old wooden boat he spoke of beaching before the winter froze it permanently afloat. She watched him from the east window picking his way down the brushy path beneath jack pines and oaks with the sun in his eyes and blue jays in the branches over his head.

He reminded her of a distant walker she had seen on the road during one of his absences. Foolishly she allowed herself to make believe this was her lover coming home, for sometimes the figure seemed to approach her, and yet other times to withdraw as if unsure or caught between commitments. The distance was so great and the tree shadows so deep across the road that for a while she couldn't be sure of his direction until some positive signal as from sunlight flashing on a face or the unmistakable shrinking of proportion which at last declared the truth.

Upon the lakeshore now he paused to roll up his pant legs before wading into the cold water. He did not hesitate, and she understood very well which way he was going—away on his sales route, away from her. First they drove into the village for sacks of groceries triple her needs for the week.

In such ways was he doting on her, creating surpluses meant to compensate for neglect he couldn't help. The kitten was a surplus. So were his phone calls. She had begun to hate his doting, but she accepted the kitten at last, just as she accepted bread that molded and potatoes whose sprouts curled into drawer corners before she could eat them. Her own direction she didn't even know, for at work within her was some process akin to the one she had partaken of upon the road, an illusory sense of moving in opposite directions at once, simultaneously toward and away from him and awaiting some positive signal to declare the truth.

That evening with the sun low behind her and with him gone away and certain to phone, she followed his morning trail to the lake. The kitten rode in a crook of her arm and clung to her shirt-front. She paused where the beached boat leaned on its side between two jack pines. Its hull was dark with wet. A green stain of lake algae like a blurry slash from a watercolor brush marked the boat's former horizon, its water beneath and its sky above. The kitten's claws pierced her shirt-front, pricking her breast. Behind her she thought for sure the phone was ringing. Inescapable were these signals to mark the beginnings and endings and entrances and exits of physical things, to mock the heart's uncertainties where no horizon or claw or dinging bell ever pertained.

Once toward summer's end he had rowed her across to a resort with a dockside beer tavern where tourists slouched on stools as though destined to slouch beneath hats with thatchy brims. Two beers they had drunk in a booth near a screen door whose slamming was their metronome. He was much like a tourist himself, she thought, though hatless and sitting erect across from her.

Like a tourist he read to her the old jokes of vulgar insinuations which are almost always to be found printed out on colored cards and tacked to the walls of tourist joints. This had given her an odd, foreign sense, for though she might have seen and read for herself all the jokes, he acted as if they were out of view from where she sat or written in a language she could not have known. Then he wished to describe for her the pickled pigs' feet and turkey gizzards shelved in gallon jars up behind the bar, the northern pike mounted on a walnut board, beef jerky in another jar, red and white plastic bobbers sold from a tossed salad bowl. He ordered a turkey gizzard with his second beer. "Two?" he asked. She shook her head.

She might have pointed out details of the tavern that he apparently missed, its dusty light fixtures and old brown furniture especially, creating here even at midday a dusky hue and the aroma of attic furniture just brought down for company, perennially put away. She didn't. He chewed his gizzard. Anyway, he was inspecting the tourists in their faded vacation attire with their fishing poles leaning in corners, lines askew.

"Aren't you glad we're not tourists?" he had asked.

"Aren't we though?" She knew before he spoke that this was the point of the tour she was given, their talk which was like postcard messages to friends at home. He missed its irony.

"No," he said, "we'll stay on after they're all gone."

On this point, she knew, he always wanted reassurance she couldn't any longer provide. A tough membrane of the gizzard lay curled on a checkered napkin before him.

The screen door slammed, and their talk had drifted to decoration of their cottage, his nearly favorite daydream of getting wallpaper from his sales stock, a pattern she could select from his sample books.

"Check with the owner first," she cautioned.

As if the owner slouched there among them, he gestured carelessly in the direction of those he considered merely tourists. "Nobody cares that much around here. You're used to city landlords and city ways."

"Joan was very easygoing about most things."

"A friend, of course, but a friend hardly counts —I mean the others, the sort people mostly rent from, the big-shot property owners."

"I lived at home before I moved in with her. That's all I was used to. My father wasn't a big-shot anything. I just happened to think that you shouldn't glue paper to somebody's walls without asking him about it first."

He waved off her contention. "And all I'm trying to say is that things don't go very much by the book around here. We'll leave the cottage better than we found it." With a single swallow he drank the last of his beer. "If we leave it," he said.

"If?"

"I've thought about buying it. When business picks up, when I get money ahead, I'll throw the owner an offer."

She couldn't recall her response, but *if* and

when he used so much that she sometimes kept count with both grim curiosity and the sort of despairing concession to tedium that sustains a tally of telephone poles from the back seat of a car on a boring trip, an accumulation of empty detail. After the interlude of wallpaper talk, he rowed her home without either of them speaking between the rap and scrape of his unpracticed oars upon the gunwale.

Now in a small town somewhere, months later, with wallpapering and buying still his day-dreams and with business no better this day and probably worse for winter's being nearer, he stood in a phone booth waiting to dote on her, prepared to think of himself as loving and atten-tive, if she would only run back two hundred feet to answer.

Now also where the tavern tourists gone, just as he predicted, and at least she remained, even if he had departed with them.

She looked out across the lake whose hues were always a bit darker than the sky and this early evening seemed barely gray while the sky was pearly in high overcast. The kitten pranced from her arms along the upright gunwale of the boat. The resort tavern she could see more clearly revealed than she had ever seen it. Its palisade of sumac, scrub oak, and hazel brush having shed its leaves, exposed there were its boat dock pulled in and stacked in sections on the empty shore, its pine siding faintly luminous under the heavy varnish, the wreck of its frostbitten geraniums in window boxes and an old washtub near a pumphouse.

Her thoughts came home to the kitten now skittering up a jack pine. To retrieve it she had to climb upon the gunwale, and while teetering there and straining to reach even its tail, she was able to forget their summer talk and his autumn phone calls. The tiny perplexity above her clawed down into her hair and eyes fragments of pine bark before it gave way to her tugging and tumbled back into her arms. A kitten was company of sorts. She would let the phone ring.

That night and three nights and mornings in succession the lake froze across to be shattered by the next day's sunlight and wind. When it froze over for good on the fourth night, jagged bits of older ice were sealed in its surface near the shore. Three inches of snow fell atop that at sunrise, melting slightly in the warmth of the day he got back to her. He tried to shovel out a skating rink, but his shovel blade struck lumps beneath the cottony snow, crevices, and the broken ice bits frozen in edgewise. Poor skating was a certainty. Still he labored an hour or more, meaning in this way to atone for his absence—one day longer than he promised—before he came to her and said, "It's hopeless."

"I haven't skated in so long, I would only fall down anyway. Must you leave tomorrow already?"

"I lost that day up north."

The kitten sipped milk and egg from a china saucer on the floor by the refrigerator. The rest of her good dishes were not yet unpacked. They had been eating on the chipped contents of their landlord's cupboard. His evasion was to ask if they might eat upon her china this night since the cat already had rated it.

"If you like," she said carelessly. "I wasn't playing favorites. My china saucers are deeper, so he doesn't spill so much."

"I'll buy a bottle of wine."

"Look, if you have to go tomorrow, you have to go. I accept that. We don't have to escape into talk about our dishes or plan parties to soothe our disappointments."

He pretended not to hear. "The stores around here don't have good wine selections, but I'll find what I can. Do you want to ride along?"

He drove into the village without her, and that night after supper on her china plates, they at last studied wallpaper samples from his stock, which was kept like a literature collection in monstrous books with dark plastic spines and board covers that had to be turned with two hands while they sat over them cross-legged on the floor. The literature of wallpaper was the inevitable rose, tulip, sugary stripe, and a pattern called Indian Paintbrush. She stared long at this one, sipping burgundy till she felt woozy and sorrowful.

"I hope I wasn't too much of a bitch this afternoon," she said with her lips on the glass and her eyes on the paper pattern. "It's just so hard, so hard sometimes." Her words went down into the glass and rippled the wine.

"Forget it; I have." He replenished his own glass from the bottle above them on the dinner table.

The pattern's semi-abstract suggestion of feathery wild rice fronds watercolored upon fabric seemed to be a runic statement of her thoughts about him, what she regarded as his better qualities splayed out upon the sheer, crisp fabric of hard facts.

"Is this the one then?" he asked. Of course he forgot himself enough, forgot her enough, to become the salesman with her. He loosened the screw post binding of his book, removed the page of Indian Paintbrush, and held it against a wall for her appraisal.

"It's the very thing," she said, though what she meant by that he wouldn't have fathomed, so she explained her choice by saying, "I've always liked wild rice" only.

"Not too busy a pattern for this room?"

"Busy, yes, but still the very thing." All this wretched *double entendre*, she felt, could sustain itself without either of them heeding it enough to devise its fresh wisecracks. It was their condition, the facts, their life together, mocking itself.

"Here, you hold it up for me now," he said, and till her arms ached, he deliberated from the right and the left and straight on from the kitchen doorway. "If that's what you want. It isn't a big seller for me, but I'm really no good at making up my mind about this sort of thing. I never can imagine what anything will look like when it's done."

He stayed with her the next day and left the morning after two hours earlier than usual to help make up lost time. Then snow fell a foot deep on the lake, wiping out his mere diagram for a skating rink. From the cottage's corners, sharply ridged drifts fanned out into broad swells between the trees. Her solitary walks among these formed paths recording her life without him for him to see when he returned. If he ever noticed, he never said. One path ran to the lake where the boat lay buried, and from there out across, for twice she tested her stamina in walking to the village. Another path she made down the driveway, which had gone unshoveled, to the road, nearly as empty as the lake during this season.

Between walks she read, composed an occasional note to Laura and Joan, never saying much to either, and watched television on an old set that had come with the cottage and like its dinnerware had cracks and chips. She made a diary on the pages of a calendar whose two-inch blank square for each day had at first appalled her by seeming to be the very truth about the time she spent here.

But as the weeks passed, she discovered to her surprise that squares filled with her tiny script increasingly outnumbered those left blank as she wrote observations about the weather and birds she had seen and kept a journal of thoughts about her circumstances. She described her life with him by writing, I *thought it would amount to more.*

In another calendar square she wrote, *I seem to leave here the placid, solitary life that he should have if he ever hopes ....* She couldn't finish this, being no longer certain what he hoped, or even if his hopes hadn't been hers alone from the beginning. So much were one's desires, like the lake beneath a summer sky, more richly hued than the facts they reflected. And only later on, when she re-read this entry, did she discover her error of writing *leave here the placid, solitary life* instead of *live here.*

She didn't correct it, for it hardly seemed an error now. With an empty square intervening she wrote, *Solitude is loneliness you can share. If you can't share it, it's just loneliness.* On December tenth, the margins filled up. *The phone rings, and I seldom answer anymore. When he comes home, he doesn't ask me why anymore. It's like a ghost is doing it. I can't believe that anyone is really calling. We both know this is hopeless, but every night he calls, and every night I'm still here. Makes no sense, fighting facts this way.* And having written that, she was certain of soon leaving him.

When he next returned, he carried a Christmas wreath decorated with a red felt bow and a dozen rolls of the Indian Paintbrush.

"For our door," he said of the wreath which

she accepted from him with both hands and held momentarily as if it were a cake while she stared down through its ring of evergreen needles framing her view of his snowy boots. He stomped them with an exuberance that seemed rehearsed. Once again he was doting, feeling good about himself for caring so much. Among the linoleum squares he left melting snow ridges. "I checked with the owner anyway," he said, "and just as I thought, he says we can do what we want here as long as we leave it as good as we found it." He dropped the wallpaper on the couch and turned back to her with several rolls tumbling off unheeded behind him.

"You'll lose your deposit. It's all opinion. He'll come when you move out and say it's worse no matter what. 'Wild rice looks crummy here', he'll say."

"Let him say it. What does it matter?" What he didn't protest this time, she noticed, as she stooped to pick up the wallpaper rolls, was the fact of moving out, of his having to leave here alone someday after she was gone, no *ifs* and *whens*. He shoved the wallpaper to one end of the couch and sat down, slouching back with his legs extended full length and his hands up behind his neck in an exaggerated pose of ease. "Merry Christmas," he said sardonically.

The next day they drove into the village to buy presents for his kids. Here too he doted, creating surpluses. He bought each of them three times what would have served beneath a Christmas tree, even from an absent father. They ran out of wrapping paper, so for the last two she used sheets cut from a roll of Indian Paintbrush. The paper was stiff and unforgiving. To make folds and corners they creased it on a table edge.

"I bought more wallpaper than we needed," he said.

She wasn't surprised to hear so.

The day before Christmas he spent with her. In a spare room where they stored things they weren't using, her dishes were repacked in boxes taped shut. Atop them were the gifts for his children. Christmas Eve at twilight he carried these out to his car, then returned as far as the door to say goodbye. The kitten purred in her arms. Around its neck she had fastened a small bell with green twine left over from their gift wrapping. She handed him the kitten.

"For your kids, another gift. I won't be able to keep him in Joan's house."

He tried to look surprised, but she knew it

was a pretense. "I'll be back tomorrow, and we'll talk this over," he said. "I'll stay the whole week this time. I've been planning on it."

"I'll be gone."

"We'll talk it over."

"It's too late," she said. "What do you think we've been talking about for the past five months?"

"Sarah, not tonight. I have to go tonight. It's Christmas Eve, for God's sake, my kids …"

"I understand that part of it," she said. "It's Christmas Eve for me too, and I can't stay here any longer. It's the same for both of us, don't you see? We both have to leave."

"I'll be back," he said again. He slammed the door, dislodging the Christmas wreath. He took the kitten. She thought she heard the tinkling of its bell.

She worked through the night and left Christmas Day well ahead of his promised return. Among the boxes and bags she couldn't carry with her she left a note asking him to ship them, and saying no more. She trudged across the lake, with an armload of parcels and her feet growing numb, just as she first imagined it on that other day they stood together by the back doorstep moving in, except that she was going away rather than coming home from the village, and she was alone, and if not happy, not entirely unhappy either.

Snow on the lake was knee-deep. She kicked through it, leaving channels rather than distinct tracks, and every one hundred yards or so she rested. Then she would gaze back at the cottage on the wooded hill, steadily retreating from her view, losing its color and finally even its form beyond a crosshatching of jack pines and oaks and —the last she saw of it—beyond what seemed an overcast. Spectral and a signal finally and all she knew of her direction.

In the village she held a flag in front of the gas station where a bus to Minneapolis stopped if anyone stood out front holding a flag, a sort of green bunting on a stick which made her think of parades and filled her with childish exuberance despite herself.

Behind her was a Christmas wreath she had lifted from a snowdrift and fastened again on the door. Behind the door were a thatchy-brimmed tourist's hat left on a closet shelf and walls she had spent the night papering with the Indian Paintbrush, a Christmas gift to him, wrapped on the inside. Her breath swirled into the air around the bunting. A gift if she was leaving her ghost at least as good as she found him.

ABOUT THE AUTHOR

James Casper has been writing ever since he was the editor of *The Loyolan,* his high school newspaper. A veteran writer now in his 8th decade, he continues to produce tastefully written novels, spellbinding short stories, and thought-provoking essays.

James was born and grew up in southern Minnesota. Apart from living in various Minnesota locales, he has resided in Boston, St. Louis, eastern Tennessee, and London, England where he finds inspiration walking along the Thames with Kate, his wife of many years. Traveling across the U.S. and Europe and writing all the while, he is most at home working at his laptop (formerly his Olympia typewriter) capturing thoughts, getting to know characters, and spinning tales that fascinate this peripatetic writer. He hopes his efforts bring you many pleasant hours of reading and reflection.

ALSO BY JAMES CASPER

Novels

An Accidental Pope: A Mystery in Five Boxes

Everywhere in Chains: Secrets of the North Shore

(and its Polish translation, Listy do Penelope)

The Far End of the Park

Short Story Collections

Turning Wind Tales: Reservation Stories

Lines That Do Not Cross: Minnesota Stories

The Casper Family

Three Hundred Years in the Life of a Family

www.ingramcontent.com/pod-product-compliance
Lightning Source LLC
Chambersburg PA
CBHW071235130626
46556CB00003B/1023